ANN TURNBULL grew up in south-east London, but moved to Shropshire with her husband and children in the 1970s. She has written books for children and young people of all ages, many of which are historical stories. Her books for young adults include *Alice in Love and War* (a story of the English Civil War) and a trilogy about the early Quakers: *No Shame, No Fear, Forged in the Fire*, and *Seeking Eden*. *No Shame, No Fear* was shortlisted for both the Guardian Fiction Prize and the Whitbread Book Award (now known as the Costa Book Award).

You can visit Ann's website at www.annturnbull.com.

IN THAT TIME OF SECRETS

In That Time of Secrets

ANN TURNBULL

SilverWood

Published in 2018 by SilverWood Books

SilverWood Books Ltd
14 Small Street, Bristol, BS1 1DE, United Kingdom
www.silverwoodbooks.co.uk

ISBN 978-1-78132-807-1 (paperback)
ISBN 978-1-78132-808-8 (ebook)

British Library Cataloguing in Publication Data
A CIP catalogue record for this book is available from
the British Library

Page design and typesetting by SilverWood Books
Printed on responsibly sourced paper

To the memory of my mother, with love

England: The West Midlands

1605

Chapter One

From my place near the window I saw a flicker of movement along the road. Could that be horsemen? The small leaded panes made it hard to be sure. No one else seemed to have noticed. I was new here, and young. I dared not raise a false alarm.

The room was full of people, all standing. Everyone was facing the altar, even those near the door who probably could not see the priest. I had a partial view, blocked by higher status servants and by a fretwork screen that separated the rest of us from Lady Chilton and her two aged aunts. Beyond them I could see Father Taberer and hear what he was saying, though I didn't understand all the Latin. There was a comforting smell of incense and beeswax; and the priest's chasuble, which was green, embroidered in gold and crimson, gleamed in the light from the windows.

I was unsure when to stand and when to kneel, so I'd been listening intently and watching people around me for clues. But now, distracted by that blink of movement among the trees, I lost my place and knelt hurriedly, treading on my skirts and stumbling against Mistress Pyatt, who gave me a sharp look.

We stood again – and I saw that I had been right: a small group of men was riding towards the house. Sunlight flashed on steel.

Armed men. On a Sunday. It could only be the pursuivants.

I had to speak. I must.

I drew breath – and then a man behind me shouted, "Soldiers! It's a raid!" and the room erupted into movement.

All the kitchen and garden servants turned to leave. They filed out without panic, moving with practised speed through the doorway and down the stairs. Those in front of me – the steward, the butler, and the secretary David Hawley – followed close behind them. Master Hawley was wide-eyed and pale. Perhaps this is new to him, I thought, as it is to me.

As people began reaching the lower floors I heard urgent talk, doors opening and shutting, fast footsteps. It set my heart jumping. But everyone else seemed calm.

The gatekeeper would now do everything he could to delay the soldiers' entry, and then the kitchen staff would bar the door until the threats to break it down forced them to open up. Father Taberer should have enough time to hide. He had already pulled off his robes. Now he scooped up the pyx, the chalice and the box of wafers, whipped off the altar cloth, bundled everything into a bag, lifted the altar stone, and hurried out. Someone snuffed the candles; another opened a window. Mistress Pyatt placed a box of silk threads and a pincushion on the altar, restoring it to its everyday function as a side table in what was now once again the sewing room.

Lady Chilton turned to me. "Mary, you and Mistress Pyatt will remain here. Take up some small piece of embroidery suitable for a Sunday. I shall retire to my chamber with a convenient headache and try to dismiss their suspicions. And Mary: if they do come up here, let Mistress Pyatt do the talking."

When she had gone I exclaimed, "Oh, I hope they won't come!"

"You have nothing to fear." Mistress Pyatt sat down, threaded a needle with green silk and began the outline of a leaf.

She was a pleasant, calm woman – a widow, forty or more and growing stout. She was in charge of linen and mending, and also of me. Since my arrival at Lyde Hall a little over a week ago I had been under her supervision.

My hands shook, and the silk thread split when I tried to pass it through the needle. I looked around me.

"Where did Father Taberer take all the things for Mass?" I asked.

"They will have gone into the hide with him. Most of the time we keep them stowed under the floorboards in here. Your chair is covering the place."

"Oh!" I could see it now: a join that was not filled with dust, near the hem of my skirts. Instinctively I put my foot over it.

From outside we heard banging on the outer door, loud voices and an answering mumble from within – gatekeeper John Frewen doing his work of obstruction. But he couldn't hold them off for long. I knew they'd have a warrant, and soon we heard them coming through into the courtyard, and there was more shouting and argument as the kitchen folk were forced to unbar the door.

They'd be angry by the time they got in.

We heard a great scraping of furniture as they moved around the stone-flagged kitchens – a crash of metal on stone, followed by shouts. And then, worse, they were coming upstairs – were on the floor below us, in Lady Chilton's room. Their manner was different with her: loud, but courteous. No shouting. The lady's voice was too quiet for me to hear.

I trembled as we waited.

Mistress Pyatt put a hand on my arm: "Here they come, now."

They were on the stairs, near – so near – knocking with their fists on walls and partitions, seeking hollow places.

"They'll find Father Taberer!"

I knew that if the priest was found he would be taken away and could face a charge of treason and a terrible death.

"He's safely hidden," she assured me.

"Where is the hide?"

"There are several. You'll find out where they all are before long. But I won't tell you now because the less you know, the less you can be made to tell."

Made to tell. The thought of that caused me to shake and drop my work. I snatched it up as a knock came on the door.

Three men entered. We both rose to our feet.

They were civil enough, but two of them immediately started poking around. My breathing quickened. I knew there were priests' vestments awaiting repairs, hidden under a pile of sheets and shirts in a basket.

The leader sniffed the air. "Candles on an August morning?"

"We were up early," said Mistress Pyatt. "It was a little dark for sewing."

"So you lit candles scented with" – he sniffed again – "incense?"

"Only beeswax, sir," she replied. "Lady Chilton will not have us use tallow anywhere except the cellars as the smell is so foul."

The man turned his attention to me. I tried to breathe steadily as he looked me up and down. "A new maid here, are you?"

I drew myself up. "A needlewoman and embroiderer, sir. I came ten days ago, at Lammastide." My heart was beating so hard I feared he must hear it.

"And your name?"

"Mary Wilshaw."

"Age?"

"Seventeen."

He frowned, and looked at a paper he carried. "We have another Wilshaw on the list for this house: Robert Wilshaw, aged twenty."

"My brother, sir."

"Your brother is manservant to Lady Chilton's son, Francis."

"Yes."

"Since when?"

"A little over a year ago."

"And you are both from Dudley? Your father is a tailor?"

"Yes."

"You are not at church this morning, Mistress Wilshaw."

"I go to church with my family when I am at home."

"But now you will become a recusant?"

"We are some distance from a church here." I looked to Mistress Pyatt for reassurance; was I right to say these things? She gave a hint of a nod. "Some distance," I repeated, "and I am new to this place. Lady Chilton will advise me what to do."

He laughed at that. "Oh, she will! She will!"

He came closer, making me flinch, and picked up my piece of embroidery: a child's kerchief decorated with some ornamental letters of the alphabet.

"This is a pretty thing. A gift?"

"Yes. For my cousin. To help her learn her letters."

I reached out, wanting it back. Mistress Pyatt caught my eye and made a small calming gesture.

He turned the scrap of linen in his hands. "Can you read, Mistress Wilshaw? English? Latin?"

"No, sir."

This was not strictly true. I could read and understand the Pater Noster and the Ave Maria and several other prayers because I knew them by heart. And I could read English well enough for simple correspondence and accounts. But I judged it wise to claim as little education as possible.

"You should learn to read English," he said. "Then you could read God's holy word for yourself and turn your back on priests and popery."

He returned the kerchief to me and I tucked it away, out of sight.

I thought he would leave me then, but instead he startled me with another question: "Where are your brother and Francis Chilton?"

"I – I don't know, sir. They have been away a day or two."

"Visiting some acquaintance of the gentleman?"

"I would not know, sir."

He gave a little sigh of acceptance. "No, I suppose you would not."

And with that, having found no proof of a Catholic Mass being said in the house, he called up his men and they left.

Mistress Pyatt turned to me and let out a breath. "You did *very* well, Mary! I never thought he would fix on you like that."

"I felt so frightened! Will it always be as bad?"

"No. And they don't come often. Though just lately…I don't know – they seem to have been springing more visits on us. We thought things would be better when the old queen died. But King James…well, it's safer not to talk. We'll stay here and sew until they are well away. Sometimes they'll seem to go and then they circle back to catch us out."

She continued to sew, though I saw her lips moving and guessed she was murmuring prayers. I picked up my work, but my mind still ran on the morning's events.

Why had the pursuivant asked about Rob and Francis Chilton? I didn't see much of my brother here. His master's chambers were in the west wing, where I had no reason to go; and it seemed the two of them were often away – and why not? Francis was still a youngish man – twenty-nine, unmarried, and fond of company and hunting.

I thought about Master Hawley, too. David. Lady Chilton's secretary. He was younger, around my brother's age. We had never spoken, but I often stole a glance at him, and I knew he was aware of me. I liked his looks.

He was mid-height; dark, strong brows; a clerk's hands, clean except for an ink-stain on the right second finger. His voice was clear and pleasing, with a Shropshire accent. I remembered his shocked expression when the alarm was raised. I'd felt that same fear myself.

When all seemed safe again and people had begun to move around, Mistress Pyatt said, "Come with me."

She led me out of the sewing room into the passage; but instead of descending by the back stairs as usual, we turned right, towards the main staircase, and went down just three steps.

"Here," she said.

She turned round and lifted up the top of the second step as if it were the lid of a desk.

Inside was a shallow tray set into the stair space. It contained a blue velvet drawstring bag with something in it. Jewellery, I supposed, or money. But why show me this?

Then, to my surprise, she knocked gently on the wooden base of the tray and said, "Father...?"

I heard Father Taberer's voice from somewhere below: "Have they gone?"

"Yes." Mistress Pyatt lifted out the tray – and beneath it I saw a large hiding place, high enough for a man to stand upright. Father Taberer was there, looking up at us.

I realised then that the tray containing the velvet bag had been put there to make any searchers think there was nothing more to be found.

Father Taberer stepped onto a ladder, climbed up, and – with some difficulty – twisted his body and squeezed out through the narrow space.

"My thanks to you both," he said, standing up and

brushing dust from his breeches. He smiled. He was a handsome man, strongly built and still young. Much of the time he dressed as a gentleman so that any chance visitor to the house would think him an acquaintance of the family, and he had no trouble passing himself off as such. "I think he enjoys the play-acting," Mistress Pyatt had told me.

The release from fear made us all light-hearted. Father Taberer laughed aloud. Lady Chilton and her maid appeared on the stairs below us, and with them was David Hawley, who broke into a great smile at the sight of Father Taberer. Lady Chilton, looking bright-eyed, said, "I am marvellously recovered from my headache. Father, shall we have a Mass this evening, since we were interrupted?"

"We shall, my lady," he agreed.

"And now I must go down," she said, "and speak to everyone."

This surprised me. I had not expected the lady to mingle with her servants. Indeed, I knew she and her family usually heard Mass in private, in their chambers. But Mistress Pyatt told me afterwards that Lady Chilton liked to bring us all together from time to time. "It bonds us," she said.

We went downstairs. The noise of voices and laughter reached us before we arrived, and I realised that no one down there was hiding their relief and excitement. Lady Chilton ordered a breakfast of bread and small beer for everyone – for the Mass had been early – and praised us for our loyalty. She also enquired about any questions that might have been asked, any places tested for priest holes, any names taken.

I said, nervously, "Their leader took my name, my lady. And he asked about…about your…"

"My son?"

"Yes! Where he and my brother were." I stopped, and felt the eyes of many people on me. Had I said too much?

"Mary behaved bravely," Mistress Pyatt said – and I felt a rush of affection for her. "The man asked her a lot of questions and she answered well."

Lady Chilton seemed grateful, but I saw anxiety in her face. Did she have reason to fear for her son? There were so many secrets in this house. I felt I knew nothing and no one. I slid a glance at David Hawley and caught him looking at me. At once I lowered my gaze.

But when Lady Chilton and Father Taberer had gone, and Master Hawley with them, I found myself drawn into the chatter and laughter in the servants' hall. It seemed that this one had been easy, as raids go.

"So there's them pushing from outside and me and Martin shoving from inside…'I have a warrant!' he says, and I tells him where he can stick it…"

The laundry woman laughed. "Remember that time when we had the priest in the hide by the bread oven for four hours? It was January and he enjoyed the warmth. I said to him, 'You must be done to a turn, Father!'"

"And when we had three priests in the attics and the sheriff's men searching and knocking everywhere," a little fair-haired maid said. "Oh! I was terrified!"

"But they never found them."

"No. Those hides are good."

"I've only seen one," I said.

"Under the stairs? That's the biggest one. They can stand up in there."

"But they can't escape," said Master Tandy, the cook. "In the attics they can move from one hiding place to another and come down a different way. Under the stairs, once they've found you there's only one way out. You're like a rat in a trap."

I shuddered. We were talking about the torture and deaths of good men.

"Well, mistress," the laundry woman turned to me, her manner deferential and yet with the superiority of someone older and more experienced, "you'll be learning all the ways of this house. Dudley you come from, isn't it?"

"And you're Master Wilshaw's sister, aren't you?" said the little fair-haired girl, whose name seemed to be Nell.

I could see she had an eye for Rob, which didn't surprise me, as my brother was always popular with our maids at home.

"And you've come to do embroidery, they say?" said the laundry woman.

"And mending, and alterations," I said. "Whatever is needed."

"But embroidery… Where did you learn that?"

"From my mother. She was here as an embroiderer before she married."

Mistress Pyatt, who had been talking to her friend, the herb woman Elizabeth White, appeared at my side. "Mary, we should go back upstairs." And as we moved off, she said, "Don't become too friendly with the kitchen and laundry folk. Young Meg Boucher is a better companion for you."

Meg was Elizabeth White's assistant. I liked her, but she was a quiet girl and Mistress White kept her busy in the still room, where the remedies were prepared.

"We all work together," Mistress Pyatt continued, "and you'll be sure to have dealings with everyone, but people will respect you more if you remember your status."

I knew she was right. But I wanted to make friends here. I didn't want to be thought high and mighty.

And that evening many of us were drawn together again when Father Taberer said another Mass after supper. At first I kept glancing out of the window at the deepening shadows along the road. What if the soldiers came back? What if they caught us this time? But all was quiet. The candles burned brightly in the dimness of the sewing room, once more transformed into a church; and as we stood there listening and taking part in the prayers, there was a feeling of thankfulness and of a shared enterprise. And when we knelt to pray, we sank to our knees as one.

Chapter Two

Lyde Hall is only five miles or so, as the crow flies, from my home in the centre of Dudley. I'd always known of it, and had seen from a distance its tall twisted chimneys rising above the trees. The house stands on a low hill above a brook and is surrounded by fields and woodland. An avenue of beeches leads to the gate, and on the day my father brought me there I had looked up and admired the great house, built of rosy brick, with its gables and leaded windows and its heavy oak door protected by a deep porch.

John Frewen had seen us coming and opened up the door in welcome, revealing a stone-flagged entrance hall and a distant glimpse of courtyard and high brick walls.

My father and I dismounted. As he turned to go I asked him, "Will I do? My gown...my hair...?" I struggled to tuck in a loose strand.

He smiled. "Of course you will! The lady asked for you especially."

She had. And I was eager to please her. When my father had gone and I was summoned to her parlour,

I approached nervously and curtseyed – and was even more intimidated to see that there were two other ladies sitting in the room, and a maid in the window seat with her needlework.

"Welcome, Mary," said Lady Chilton. "How like your mother you are! She was an embroiderer here long ago, when I was a young bride – an excellent needlewoman. I have seen some of your work, so I know she has taught you well."

The lady looked to be a strong, energetic woman, with a straight, unsmiling yet friendly manner. I felt that she knew and oversaw everything that happened in her house. She introduced her two companions, who I now saw were both very old. They were aunts of hers, and their names were Lady Vavasour (mild-faced with milky blue eyes) and Lady Warne (sharp and alert). The lady's maid in the window seat was Jane Shenton.

So many new names to remember! I took a breath to calm myself.

"I hear that your father is the most sought-after tailor in Dudley," said Lady Chilton. "You must be proud of him."

"I am, my lady."

"But I think it is difficult for your family to hear Mass regularly?"

"It is. My father can't afford to pay the recusancy fines."

"So you go to church?"

"Yes. Sometimes a travelling priest comes secretly to our house – but not often. It's so dangerous."

"But you would like to hear Mass?"

"Oh, yes! I would."

That clearly pleased her. "Let me tell you about Lyde Hall," she said.

I was surprised. I had expected merely a few questions about my needlework skills, followed by a quick dismissal. But I remained standing still, as was proper, with my gaze lowered. The lady leaned forward a little in her chair, and I sensed that we were coming to the most important part of this interview. "At Lyde Hall we are always very careful in our choice of servants," she said. "Not only must they be trustworthy, they may need courage in the face of threats and interrogation. Loyalty is essential. You know we are recusants – that we refuse to attend the Protestant church?"

"I do, my lady."

"You will be able to hear Mass regularly, and to make confession if you wish. A priest lives here: Father Taberer. He passes as my cousin. And we have other priests staying here from time to time. We are known as a safe house."

She began talking about the past; about King Henry, who had made himself head of the English church and broken with Rome…good Queen Catherine cast aside and divorced…the defacing of holy statues…the destruction of the monasteries…centuries of faith and tradition swept away so that King Henry could marry his Protestant whore…

I had heard all this many times from my parents and others, and so, while I listened, I let my eyes take in the room. A little white dog sat at the lady's feet – so still I hadn't seen it till then; a tabby cat was purring on Lady Vavasour's lap. I noticed the embroidered cushions and curtains, sumptuous yet faded; the lattice windows – one of them open; a breeze stirring tendrils of fair hair around Jane Shenton's face as she sat sewing…

"I remember it." A different voice.

One of the old gentlewomen had spoken: Lady Warne, the sharper-looking one. "I was five years old, six maybe. I saw those men go into the church with their hammers and chisels to chip stone, and their pikes to break the windows…"

She was talking about the destruction in King Henry's time – so long ago, and yet she remembered it. I gazed at her, astonished.

"They smashed the stained glass windows, and they hacked the faces and hands from the saints. I cried – I was frightened – when I saw a row of saints, all faceless. And the Virgin, broken on the floor."

"And then the whitewash," said the other aunt. "The holy pictures on the walls, painted over. All lost."

I almost spoke out then; almost said, "No – not all." I was remembering our parish church in Dudley and the place at the wall end of a pew where I always sat. There, between the base of the wall and an oak upright, where the whitewash petered out in rough brush strokes, you could see a woman's shoe, and over it the folds of a robe – green with a black and gold border, looped up over a kirtle of faded rose. The end of a gold belt or tassel hung down, and higher up was the trace of a hand. A saint, my mother said. But which one? As a child I'd loved this secret saint; she was my favourite, whoever she was. But no one knew.

Lady Chilton looked around the room, drawing in the aunts, Jane, and me. "So, you see, Mary, here at Lyde Hall my son and I have a duty to uphold the true faith in England until such time as it comes into its own again – as it surely will. We have the means, the connections, and this house itself, which can shelter priests in secrecy and safety. And we are not alone. We are part of a web of great houses, many of them nearby. The Jesuits' mission is to train priests for England, and *our* mission – all of us here – is to help them in every way we can." She turned to me then with a hint of a smile. "Even to repairing their vestments."

My interview was over.

I had not thought about church vestments, but of course Lady Chilton kept some hidden, for use by visiting priests. Later, Father Taberer showed me, with some pride, his own lightweight embroidered silk robes that he found so convenient for a life of travel and secrecy. His was a green set, and he relied on his hosts to provide the other seasonal colours when they could.

It was one of Lady Chilton's stock – a red chasuble embroidered in gold and purple – that I was working on three days after the excitement of our interrupted Mass. Mistress Pyatt was busy with a torn lace cuff belonging to Francis Chilton, while I stood with the voluminous scarlet robe supported on a table, repairing a section of worn embroidery. I had told Lady Chilton that I could repair old embroideries so that the mending wouldn't show, so I knew I was being tested and was determined to please her. But it was tiring work. I was glad when the laundry woman, Kate Newey, bumped open the door of the sewing room with her hip and set down a large basket of washed and ironed clothes on the floor.

"I've brought you some linen." She sighed dramatically.

"Those stairs – they'll be the death of me! Your brother's back, Mary."

"Rob!" I had so much to tell him – and to ask him. I wanted to hear all his news. I pushed my needle into the pincushion, stretched my arms and gazed across the room to rest my eyes. The sunlight was in the west window now. We'd already had the best of the light for sewing.

"Came in just now, they did." Kate Newey, ignoring Mistress Pyatt's little sigh that I knew meant, 'Thank you, Kate. Now go back to your own duties', sidled over to me and looked at what I was doing. It was a repair to a design of twining leaves and chalices in gold and green, the details picked out with tiny pearls. Kate's rough, reddened hand hovered longingly over the rich threads.

"This is beautiful," she said, gazing at my work with something like awe.

"I am only mending it," I said. "Here...and around this pattern... See?"

"It'll never show," she said, almost reverently.

"It'll never be done," said Mistress Pyatt, "unless Mary is left in peace to work on it."

This time there was no mistaking the hint, and Kate said, "Well, I'd best be off."

She went out, and we heard her plodding down the stairs.

I took up my work again. But I was restless now, knowing that Rob was back.

"Run down and see your brother, if you want to," said Mistress Pyatt.

"Oh! May I? But you said—"

"I merely wanted Kate to go. She is too familiar. You

are not a scullery maid for her to chat to." She smiled. "Go – before I change my mind!"

Mistress Pyatt had already begun using me to save her own legs – sending me with messages for Kate Newey, or to fetch small beer, or cushions; or to the herb woman for a salve for her hands. I was willing enough. At home I'd been accustomed to being busy in and around the house and having freedom to wander. And I was curious about everything.

"Shall I bring something from the kitchen?" I asked.

"A nibble, yes. If you will." Mistress Pyatt enjoyed sweetmeats.

I stepped out into the passage. A door on the wall opposite led into one of the spare bedchambers – a run of three small rooms that were kept ready for use by higher status male servants or visiting priests.

"Those three rooms have connecting doors," Mistress Pyatt had told me when I first arrived, "and there's a way up to the attic hides in one of them. They are the safest rooms for priests."

"But Father Taberer doesn't sleep up here, does he?"

"No. He lives permanently at Lyde Hall – well, as permanently as a Jesuit priest lives anywhere these days. He's a gentleman by birth and has one of the better chambers on the first floor. But the secretary – young Master Hawley – he has one of those rooms."

I knew now which one was David Hawley's. It was the third door along, the furthest from the sewing room.

It had taken me several days to begin to find my way around, and I still sometimes became lost. My own home – my parents' house and workshop in Dudley – was a substantial place with a wide frontage, but its design was simple. It was a town house, two-storey, with only one staircase and no passages: the rooms led off one from another. Here at Lyde Hall there were rooms within rooms, half-landings with locked doors on them, hidden passages, layers of life: an outer, grand way of living, and an intense, secret inner life.

I descended the narrow, twisting staircase that led to the kitchen passage and found my way out to the yard and over to the stables.

Rob was there, brushing down one of the horses while a stable boy tended to the other. Fine horses, these were, not like the carriers' horses we'd see in our yard at home. When I appeared, the boy bobbed his head to me and led his animal slightly away, to give us privacy.

"Mary!" Rob paused in his brushing and came to kiss me.

His face was cool, and smelt of fresh air and some perfume such as gentlemen use. I wrinkled my nose. We'd teased him about smelling of perfume when he came home to Dudley on his last visit.

He grinned as he began brushing again. He was a pleasing young man – even I admitted it – with crooked front teeth that somehow added to his charm. And he wasn't cut out to be a tailor. Our elder brother, Mark, had taken on that role, and worked in the family business. Rob was different. I saw how he was caught up in this new life; it delighted him, serving Francis Chilton, moving among the gentry. He had fine clothes, money, responsibility. It seemed he was making his way in the world.

The boy had stabled the other horse and gone. Even so, I lowered my voice when I asked, "Where have you been?"

"Oh – a grand house." I noticed that he did not give its name. "South of here. Good food. Good hunting. Visitors coming and going all the time."

He's not going to tell me anything, I thought.

But then he noticed my disappointment and began to talk about things he knew would interest me or make me laugh: a pompous servant whose ways had amused him; a pretty maid he'd danced with; the fine clothes of the gentlefolk (he knew I loved to hear about clothes). There was a dog he'd taken to: "Game little thing, great shiny eyes, so eager – wish I could have kept him. I miss our Gilly."

"Oh, I do, too!" I said. "But I'm glad to be here."

"Are you, our wench?"

I smiled at the homely endearment, but he looked earnestly at me.

"You're pleased I recommended you to her ladyship?"

"Yes, of course! But, Rob – we had a raid on Sunday. During Mass."

"I know. John Frewen told me."

"The pursuivants' leader asked me about you and your master; where you were."

He frowned. "Some stickler for the law, then. The Five Mile rule."

"Oh!" I hadn't thought of that. But I knew it meant that Francis Chilton would need to apply for a licence whenever he wanted to travel more than five miles from home.

"Because he is a recusant?" I said.

For the first time I realised how restricting that law must be. No doubt the licence had to be paid for. And the authorities would know where you were going, and when, and for how long.

"But he must have family further away than that!" I said. "And many friends. The great houses he visits…"

"Shh!" He nodded agreement, but signalled to me to lower my voice. "Mostly the authorities don't check. Especially a mile or two over. They can't be everywhere. And some of them are sympathetic and turn a blind eye."

"That man that spoke to me – *he* would check," I said. I remembered his intimidating manner; how he'd sprung that question on me.

"Then be careful what you say, and who hears you."

"I didn't know anything. I told him I didn't."

"Good. The less you know the better."

"Mistress Pyatt said that, too."

"She's right."

But *you* like having secrets, I thought. You enjoy this life: the danger, the intrigue, being your master's right-hand man.

Later, coming back up from the kitchen with some sweet pastries for Mistress Pyatt tucked into a fold in my apron, I reached the top of the stairs and almost collided with David Hawley, who was standing outside the sewing room door with his hand raised, as if about to knock.

"Oh!"

"I'm sorry…"

"No – my fault…"

We stood gazing at each other. His eyes were a warm hazel brown. My heart beat fast. I felt as if I'd been caught out in something. But if I had, it was only a wish.

"Mistress Wilshaw…" A flush spread up his face. "I came to…"

I saw a linen shirt hanging over his arm.

"For mending?" I asked.

"Yes. I thought, as it's clean, and your workroom is here, I would bring it straight to you."

"Of course." I felt warm and flustered as I took the shirt from him. "What needs doing?" I asked.

We were standing close together. His hand almost touched mine as he showed me where the sleeve gathering had come unstitched. Unlike Rob, he did not smell of perfume, but pleasantly enough of ink, and beer, and the herbs we used for clothes storage. I liked standing here with him in this enclosed space. The passage was narrow, without windows, and already it was growing dark. Soon a servant would come by with a taper and light the candles in the wall sconces.

"If you have time...?" he said.

"Oh, yes! It won't take long. I'll do it tomorrow."

"Thank you." He hesitated, as if he wanted to say more. But then he wished me good day and turned towards his room.

I went into the sewing room, which was still full of natural light.

"Who was that you were talking to?" asked Mistress Pyatt.

"Oh, just Master Hawley. He gave me a shirt for repair."

I bent over the mending basket to hide my face, for fear I was blushing. And I pushed David Hawley's shirt well down, out of sight. I was determined to be the one who mended it tomorrow.

"I brought you some tarts," I said, to distract her. I took out the napkin and opened it. "Master Tandy has been experimenting, and he wants to know which ones you like best. There is apple; plum and ginger; plum with angelica…"

"Oh…"

They all looked pretty, dusted with costly sugar and decorated with flower petals.

"The plum and ginger is good," she said later, brushing crumbs from her lips. "Have one yourself, Mary."

We had a pile of mending to sort out the next morning: worn hose to be darned, mostly; lace edgings to re-attach; and garments to be embroidered with their owners' initials.

"You'd like to do the initials, I imagine?" Mistress Pyatt said – no doubt wishing to spare me the endless darning of stockings.

"Yes," I said, thinking quickly. And as we divided up the linen, I took David Hawley's shirt and said, "I'll put initials on this one too; I see it doesn't have any." And I moved it to my own pile of work.

And when it's done, I thought, I'll take it back to him myself. No need to trouble the maids.

Chapter Three

David Hawley's shirt was well-made, I noted the next morning, as I took up the sleeve gathering and reinserted it into the shoulder seam. A simple design in good quality linen, such as I'd often made at home for my brothers. I wondered where his family lived, and who had made *this* shirt.

The repair finished, I turned my attention to the initials. He had not asked for initials, but I knew the laundry maids wanted them on everything. Lady Chilton and her son both had elaborate monograms that I had found interesting to embroider, but David Hawley's would be a simple "DH" in matching linen thread. I began working it near the hemline.

When it was done, I looked for a way to take the shirt back to him myself.

It was late morning, and I knew he often came up to his room at about this time, before going to dinner, which for the upper servants such as us was served in the great hall. Mistress Pyatt and I always went down together, and she liked to be prompt. I waited, willing David to come by. As soon as I heard footsteps in the passage and a door opening, I jumped up.

"That'll be Master Hawley. I'll take this shirt back to him before we go down."

And I hurried out.

His door was pulled to, but not shut. I tapped softly.

"Come in."

I pushed the door open.

My quick glance around the room took in the curtained bed, a washstand, and a table cluttered with books and writing materials.

David stood on the far side of the room, with his back to the door. He'd been washing his hands, but now he turned round, and I saw his eyes brighten at the sight of me.

"Mary – I mean, Mistress Wilshaw."

"You may call me Mary," I said. "I brought your shirt."

I did not step over the threshold, but let him come to me. "I've added your initials – for the laundry."

"My initials?" For a moment I thought he looked alarmed.

"Did I do wrong? I can take them out."

"No, no." He took the shirt from me and looked at my work. "It is well done. Thank you."

A look went between us, and I thought: he does like me; and I like him and want to know him better.

He laid the garment on the bed. "Will you walk down to the hall with me?"

"Yes," I said, "if we can wait for Mistress Pyatt?"

"Of course."

I was still on the threshold. I knew he wanted to

ask me in, but could not because that would seem improper. Instead, with an eye on the sewing room door, where Mistress Pyatt would appear, he asked me how I liked working for Lady Chilton, and I said that I was honoured to do so, and that it hardly seemed like work since I was doing what I enjoyed most.

"Mending torn shirts?"

"Embroidery! I hope to improve my skills and do some work of my own design if Lady Chilton will allow me."

Then I fell silent, embarrassed. A girl should not talk about herself too much, and especially not about her ambitions. "How long have you been working here?" I asked him.

"I arrived a few days before you."

"Oh!" So we were both newcomers, as I'd guessed on the day of the raid. "When the soldiers came – did that pursuivant cross-examine you, as he did me?"

"Yes. But he didn't ask many questions. I told him I come from Shrewsbury, from a Catholic family who attend the Protestant church."

"And that satisfied him?"

"I think so. He must know that Catholics hang together. And that is no crime." He turned the conversation back to me. "You will be missed at home, won't you? Especially by your mother."

"Yes. But my mother has maidservants and a sewing woman to help her. And she believes it is good for me to be here."

"She's right, I'm sure. You could not be in a better place." He spoke with feeling.

"And you?" I asked. "Will your mother miss you?"

My question was meant to tease him. Sons, of

course, are expected to leave home, and Shrewsbury is not too far away for visits on feast days and holidays. I was surprised to see a shadow cross his face: a look of grief, perhaps, or even guilt. But almost at once he smiled and said, "She is pleased to have me settled here. I am of age now – turned twenty-one this summer."

"I'm seventeen," I said. "Do you have brothers and sisters?"

"An elder brother. He's a physician, like my father."

"But you…?"

"I wanted something different."

"To work in a recusant household?"

"Yes—"

He suddenly straightened up – he'd been leaning with an arm against the doorpost, close to me. I realised he must have seen Mistress Pyatt emerge from the sewing room, and I turned round to face her.

"There you are!" she said, raising her eyebrows. "Shall we go down – all three of us?"

And so we walked down to the great hall on the ground floor and joined the people going in through the door at the lower end. Everyone was there except the maids and the kitchen servants.

I had not yet grown accustomed to eating in such a grand, public space. At home I would help our maids set the table, bring in dishes, clear away afterwards. And there would be perhaps seven or eight of us in a cosy panelled room, with the dog, Gilly, running around, wanting titbits.

There were dogs here in the hall at Lyde, but in every other way the occasion was much more formal. The hall was spacious, with high leaded windows and shields and coats of arms hanging on the dark panelled walls. The table had been set all down its length with plates, bowls, cups and spoons. There were baskets of small loaves, and bowls of herb-scented water for washing fingers. I glanced at the high end of the table and caught the glint of silver and Venetian glass, but here at the lower end we had pewter. All the men sat on one side, the women on the other, and there was a hierarchy of seating. David sat above, but next to, the two musicians, Ambrose and Henry, and I was across the board from him, beside Mistress Pyatt. My brother was higher up the table, below the steward, and looking pleased to find himself opposite pretty Jane Shenton. I shook my head at Rob. Jane was a gentlewoman, far above his station.

The family arrived last. Lady Chilton took her seat at the high end, her son next to her, and on her other side the two ancient kinswomen in old-fashioned ruffs. Next to Francis was Father Taberer, dressed in lay clothes. We all rose, and bowed or curtseyed to them as they came in and took their places.

I tried not to look at David during that meal, but couldn't resist glancing across the table. Once or twice I caught his gaze on me and looked quickly away, but most of the time he was talking animatedly with the two musicians, so I was able to watch the three of them unobserved. I knew that both Ambrose and Henry played lute and viol, and sometimes I had heard them singing and playing somewhere downstairs – probably in the great chamber or the lady's parlour. Ambrose was older and quieter, Henry slight, red-haired and lively. I could see that David liked Henry; they laughed a lot and had plenty to say to each other.

Mistress Pyatt nudged me. "Keep your eyes on *this* side of the table."

I realised I had been watching the young men for some time, and quickly withdrew my gaze. Mistress Pyatt never talked much at meal times, preferring to concentrate on her dinner – but she was always aware of what was going on around her.

Various dishes were passing along the table, and I intercepted a small trout and some bread – good bread, but not the manchet that was being eaten higher up the table. I had developed a liking for manchet, having sometimes been given leftover pieces for Mistress Pyatt and myself when I went down to fetch our supper.

At last there came a rustling and movement throughout the room, signalling the end of the meal. Mistress Pyatt and I stood up and bobbed curtseys as the gentlefolk left the hall. We all filed out – and I looked quickly across at David again and saw with a rush of pleasure that he was looking at me. Then we were separated as everyone left, and Mistress Pyatt and I turned towards the back stairs and made our way up to the second floor.

"Oh, that cat!" she exclaimed as we entered the sewing room.

A small grey tabby cat opened yellow eyes and regarded us from the mending basket, where it had been curled up asleep.

"Out!" she said.

The cat looked wary, but did not move.

I picked it up. It clung to my sleeve with sharp claws, and I stroked its head.

Mistress Pyatt tutted as she shook out the top layer

of linen from the basket. "Fur, dirt – probably fleas as well… It must have sneaked in when I left for dinner. Oh, put it out, Mary!"

I took the creature to the door and dropped it in the passage, by the stairs.

Back in the sewing room, she told me, "This room always attracts the cats. It's the sunny windowsills and the baskets of linen." She looked out of the window. "We could sit outside and sew this afternoon. You take the basket, and I'll gather up the other things. We'll find an arbour seat."

It was good to go outside. Lyde Hall had several gardens: the herb garden; a private formal garden used only by the gentlefolk; an orchard; and a larger garden with paths, flowers and arbours where any of us could walk or sit to do our work in fine weather.

We found that the garden already had inhabitants: the herb women, Elizabeth and Meg, were spreading leaves and flowers on frames to dry in the sun. We sat nearby, under an arched trellis, and talked as we worked. I discovered that Meg – a soft-spoken, careful girl of about my own age – was an orphan brought up by Elizabeth, her aunt.

"We don't live at the Hall," Meg explained. "Our home is on the edge of Lyde village, but we come in most days."

The two of us began talking together about how different our childhoods had been – she so quietly raised and I with my brothers and the busy shop. But we were interrupted by a commotion from the yard: men's voices, laughter, clatter, and the sound of the side gate into the meadow being opened.

All four of us stood up. A large wooden frame was moving past the garden gate, borne by two of the men.

"They are setting up the butts – for archery practice!" said Elizabeth.

"In the meadow?"

The side wall of the garden lay alongside the meadow. Meg and I ran to this wall, which was above head-height and built of brick.

"We can't get up there," said Meg. She was small and slight and, unlike me, had not had boys to play with.

"Yes, we can."

I found footholds somehow, using tree roots and damaged bricks, and climbed up, hauling Meg – protesting and laughing – after me, and so brought our heads above the parapet. David was there, in the meadow, with Rob, Henry, Ambrose, Martin the cook's assistant, the two stable lads, and even John Frewen – who was surely too old to be required by law to practise archery but who looked as ready as the young ones.

Henry spotted us, and spoke to Rob, and the two of them swept off their hats and performed mock bows, making us laugh; and then David saw us, and also tipped his hat.

"Girls! Don't make such a show of yourselves!" exclaimed Mistress Pyatt – though she and Elizabeth were laughing at us, so we took no notice.

"Your brother shoots well," said Meg, her gaze following Rob as he stepped back from a bull's-eye and acknowledged the shouts of approval.

Peering further round, I saw the maidservants – Barbara, Nell and Alice – perched on the low wall of the herb garden, watching and clapping.

Henry was next. He showed no skill whatsoever, but seemed happy to be laughed at.

When David stepped up, I gave him my close attention. He was intent and focused, but his first shot went wide of the mark. The second was better.

Next up was John Frewen, the gatekeeper. The old man moved with surprising grace and confidence and hit the mark every time. The kitchen folk clapped and shouted approval. Clearly he was their champion.

"Perhaps he was a soldier," I said.

"Meg! Mary!" Elizabeth called us down.

We were growing tired of clinging on with our fingers, and this time we obeyed, brushing dust from our hands and skirts.

Later, when Mistress Pyatt and I had returned to the sewing room, and the evening light was slanting into the room, I went downstairs to fetch our supper. There was cold meat, plums, and some small manchet loaves left over from the gentlefolks' meal. As I reached the top floor landing carrying my full tray, David emerged from his chamber. I realised he must have been listening for me.

"Oh – manchets!" he exclaimed. "Are there any left?"

I set down the tray on the small table outside the sewing room door. "No. These were the last. But have one."

"May I?" He took one of the soft white loaves and broke it in half. "I like these. Here…" He handed me the other half.

I took it, and we stood eating and regarding one another.

"Well, you must have laughed at me this afternoon – and at Henry," he said, brushing crumbs from his clothes.

"*You* were not so bad."

"You and the herb woman's girl…?"

"Meg."

"You and Meg were distracting – disembodied heads bobbing above the wall."

I smiled. "We couldn't resist watching."

"I'll forgive you since you brought the manchets."

"Haven't you had any supper?" I asked.

"Oh, yes. I ate with Henry and Ambrose earlier, but we had no such fine bread."

"I think Master Tandy saves it for Mistress Pyatt. And I'd better go, and take this to her."

I picked up my tray.

"You look rosy," said Mistress Pyatt as I came in.

"The sunshine…" I patted my warm face.

She smiled and shook her head at me.

That day was followed by two weeks of fine, sunny weather. Everyone spent more time outside, even the kitchen folk and the maids, when they could manage it. Several times I saw David accompany Lady Chilton into the private garden, carrying a portable desk and writing materials. Sometimes Father Taberer went with them, and once or twice I saw David and Father Taberer together in one of the arbours in the main garden, sitting with books and papers about them, in what seemed to be earnest conversation. I wondered what they talked about. Could David be acting as secretary to the priest as well as to Lady Chilton? I knew the Jesuits had contacts everywhere and that secret messages must go between them. I had a feeling I should not ask David about this, but it intrigued me; I wanted to know everything about him.

The musicians sometimes came into the garden to practise, and we would sew as they sang and played, and join in with familiar choruses. Then one day they began playing a jig, and we all started tapping our feet. To my astonishment Mistress Pyatt stood up and danced a few steps on the path, and Elizabeth White joined her.

"We need some men!" said Elizabeth.

Henry put down his viol, leaving Ambrose playing, and went off to find some. He returned with Rob, Martin and David.

"Oh! Now we have a set!" exclaimed Mistress Pyatt. Henry bowed to her, and Rob to Meg, who blushed and smiled at being chosen. To my relief (for I didn't want him to single me out), David chose Elizabeth, and I partnered Martin. Not that it mattered, since we changed partners all through the dance – and with the confined space and the unevenness of the brick path and herb lawn underfoot, we were soon bumping into each other and laughing till it hurt. Young Ben from the stables appeared with a flute, Ambrose and Henry switched places, and Henry struck up a new tune, so that everyone took a turn dancing. And yet, in some way, I was dancing only with David – touching hands, curtseying, holding his gaze as we turned – as if an invisible thread drew us together.

We did three more dances, each more romping than the last, and then Martin and Ben went off to the kitchen and came back with cups and a jug of small beer. We all sat down, laughing and breathless, and Mistress Pyatt said, "Oh, I haven't danced like that for a long time!"

"Well, if you want some more, there's the village wake starts tomorrow," said Elizabeth.

"Oh!" I glanced at David, and, with a catch of breath, Meg looked at Rob. He smiled, and the colour rose in her face.

Elizabeth turned to me and asked, "Do you like wakes, Mary? Music and dancing? Fairings? They always have one in late August – in the meadow."

"Are we allowed to go?"

"Yes, we go every year. Meg and I will go on Saturday. And you'll come, won't you, Master Wilshaw?"

Rob nodded. "Of course."

"It's not a rough sort of wake," she explained to me, "just a small village fair – though they do have wrestling and cock-fighting. But we'll go soon after noon and come away before it gets rowdy."

"I'll come," I said, "if Mistress Pyatt allows it."

"We can go together," said Mistress Pyatt.

"And you, Master Hawley?" asked Elizabeth.

"Perhaps. If the lady permits it," he said guardedly – and I could not be sure what he wanted.

But I knew what *I* wanted. I wanted him to go with me to the wake, and dance with me, and walk back with me along the field paths to the hall as the moon was rising, and...

"Well, Mary, back to work," said Mistress Pyatt, as the company began to break up. She turned to Henry. "Master Gale, you may play us something soothing to sew by, if you will."

Chapter Four

On Saturday, as soon as our work was finished for the afternoon, I hurried to the bedchamber I shared with Mistress Pyatt. It was further along the passage, almost opposite the top of the grand staircase, its doorway hidden from view by a flight of four steps that curved up and around to a little half-landing between the second and attic floors. This house contained many such oddities, and I wondered if our room had once been a priest's hide or a secret chapel. It was tiny and low-ceilinged, with only one small window overlooking a courtyard, and it could never be aired sufficiently for our liking. Instead, we shook out the clothes and bedding regularly and scattered fresh herbs around.

I shared the bed with Mistress Pyatt, and hung my spare gown and my cloak from hooks on the walls. Linen and other belongings, including my treasured green shoes, were kept in a small chest near the bed. Not that I had brought many things. "Don't pack too much," my mother had advised. "Lady Chilton prefers modesty in her servants. And she likes to bestow gifts." I had got around this by bringing hidden finery: three embroidered shifts and some patterned stockings.

Now, in readiness for the village wake, I pulled out the dark lacing from my blue wool bodice. Mistress Pyatt came in as I was threading a yellow lace through the holes.

"You're wasting your pretty things," she warned. "The fields will be muddy and they're a rough lot in the village. You'll get jostled."

"I *know*." It was like having my mother around – and I took as little heed. My imagination had leapt ahead to the wake, the dancing, David. He had told me yesterday he would be there. I needed to be beautiful, mud or not.

I unpinned my hair, shook it down and combed it, then coiled and re-pinned it and put on a fresh cap.

We set off together. The afternoon was warm, the fields full of people. Smoke blew across to us from a pig roasting over a great fire, and people were crowding around, burning their fingers as they snatched at the hot meat, and drinking beer. Some musicians started up – fiddlers, their elbows going like saws; and a circle of dancers, many of them children, was formed with much tugging and laughter. The field was all over molehills and my shoes were soon muddy. Mistress Pyatt drew me with her to some stalls spread enticingly with ribbons and thread, bead necklaces, cheap lace and flowers. Women congregated there, and we met Elizabeth and Meg and some of the maids.

I'd once loved to look at stalls like these, but now, working every day with silks and gold thread and the finest linen, I was spoilt for such trifles, and could only see how tawdry they were. Besides, my mind was on other things. I gazed out across the field, hoping to see David.

Surely he would come? Meg was looking around too, no doubt in search of my brother. Several of the younger men from the hall were there, enjoying the opportunity to talk to the girls and seize hold of them in the dances.

Beyond the pig roast, a cockfight was in progress. Men were shouting, punching the air, their voices ugly. I looked away, certain that David would not be there. But on the outskirts of that noisy crowd I saw two men talking together. I recognised Ben Truelove, one of the grooms – then, with a shock, saw that the other man was the pursuivant who had questioned me. What were they talking about? Were they friends? I doubted it. Ben was just a lad, and a mere servant; and he was moving away now, shaking his head. Why was the pursuivant here? He surely did not live in the village. He turned then, and saw me, and I knew he had recognised me. He made a move in our direction, and in alarm I turned to Meg and said, "Let's go and dance!"

We joined hands, ran and broke into the circle, where we quickly picked up the simple steps.

The music changed, and now we took partners for a greetings dance. My first partner was a little lad; but two partners later, when we all moved on, I found myself facing the pursuivant.

How did he get here so fast? I felt more angry than afraid.

"Mary Wilshaw," the man said, and smiled, clearly pleased with himself for remembering my name.

I would not ask him his own name, but he told me, with a small bow: "Thomas Jevons."

I could see no way to escape him now without seeming ill-mannered. He had firm hold of my arm, and he danced well, despite the tussocky field surface. Dancing with him would have been a pleasure had his presence not made me so uneasy.

He swung me around, and I thought: what does he want of me? And why isn't David here?

Partners changed again, and I was glad when Thomas Jevons handed me on to a whiskery farmhand whose breath smelt of beer and whose feet were always in the wrong place. I forgave him his clumsiness because he was not the pursuivant, and we laughed as we stumbled through the steps.

But this was hardly the afternoon I had longed for. The sky had clouded over, the breeze had turned chilly, and now a few spots of rain fell. I moved on in the dance twice more, and across the circle I saw Thomas Jevons watching me.

The dance ended. I dropped hands with my partner and glanced about, thinking of Meg. I spotted her near the stalls, with Elizabeth. So Rob had not come, either; and he'd promised he would. I felt angry with both young men, and was about to go to Meg and say so – but then I saw David.

He was walking across the field from the hall, alone. My spirits soared and I forgot all modesty and hurried to meet him.

I had to force myself to slow down, not to seem eager, or appear to have singled him out. But he strode across the field straight towards me, and I knew he was drawn to me in the same way and that our paths must inevitably meet.

We stood facing each other, and smiled.

"I thought you would not come."

"I was detained by the lady and Father Taberer."

We both looked back at the crowds around the stalls, the smoke rising from the pig roast. A sudden roar of male voices burst from somewhere out of sight, and I knew the wrestling had begun.

"Do you want to go back there?" he asked.

I hesitated. What I wanted was to stay with him.

"It's not much of a fair," I said. "And that pursuivant is there. He came and spoke to me. He remembered my name."

David's expression became wary. "I think you'd rather stay away, wouldn't you?" he said. "Shall we walk down there by the brook instead?"

I looked across to the brook, where there were willows and long grasses – a place where we could linger and talk.

"Yes," I said. There was nothing I would like more.

I glanced back as we walked, wondering whether anyone was watching us; but there was no sign of Thomas Jevons, nor of anyone from Lyde Hall. I was sure our walking away together would not go unnoticed, but I didn't mind. Why should I? There was no wrong in the two of us meeting in plain view.

Willows hung low over the water, and David held up trailing branches to let me pass beneath. Ducks and moorhens paddled in the shallows, and at sight of us a swan turned and sailed towards the bank. From here the sounds and smells of the wake were distant, and I felt free, away from the closeness of my new life at the hall, where so many duties kept me indoors.

"You don't mind missing the wake?" I asked David.

"No. Fresh air is all I need. It's a relief from too much

writing and study. Shall we walk along to the bridge?"

"Yes."

"Or run?"

I laughed. "Yes!"

I scampered with him along the muddy path.

We reached the bridge and stopped to catch our breath.

"What are you studying?" I asked.

I had thought him simply a clerk to Lady Chilton, and perhaps also to Father Taberer, but now I remembered the pile of books in his room.

"Religion and philosophy," he said. "Father Taberer is instructing me."

"In the Catholic faith?"

"Yes."

I felt there was more to it than that; but if there was, he did not seem eager to tell me. Instead, we leaned together on the parapet of the bridge and watched the ducks, busy with their constant search for food. And at his request I pointed out to him the landmarks around us: the tower of Dudley Castle; the church spire at Wombourne; Holbeach House ("You can't see it, but it's not far away – behind those trees"); and the great area of open forest that was Dudley Wood and Pennsnett Chase.

"And Dudley is where your family lives?" he said.

"Yes." And I began telling him about my life at home as a child, about my two older brothers, how they used to tease me and play tricks on me, and how I would run after them, wanting to join in their games. "See the smoke rising here and there in the chase?" I said. "That's charcoal burners. They make clearings all over. And other men, miners, dig for coal and leave pits that get covered over with leaves. I fell in one, once.”

“Into a pit!”

“It wasn’t deep, and I landed on a pile of leaves – though my brothers had to haul me out. Oh, my mother was cross! ‘Running wild’, she said. She reined me in after that.”

He laughed and told me about going to school with his brother; the masters who beat them regularly to improve their memories; how he’d liked studying despite school. And the days they spent playing in the countryside, stealing birds’ eggs, fishing, making dams in streams.

We saw sticklebacks in the water and went down for a closer look. He caught one in his hands, let it flick and wriggle and leap free to swim swiftly downstream. We saw the blue flash of a kingfisher. And I picked strands of watercress and yellow rocket flowers and studied them, noting the number of petals and stamens, their varying shades of yellow and white, the angle at which the leaves were attached to the stems. Flowers can be copied from samplers, but I like to look at them growing wild. These would make a good border pattern.

We splashed around and got muddy like children, and then clambered back up the bank as the sky darkened and thunder rumbled far off.

I dried my hands on my skirt. “Look!” I said. “It’s raining over Wombourne.”

You could see the rain as a veil of fine lines. Behind it, the sky was ominous.

“We should get back,” he said, as drops began to fall; and we ran up the field and into the shelter of a large oak, where we stood still and looked out at the gathering storm.

The rain was falling heavily now; the sky was full of it, and distant thunder rolled around. Shrieks and shouts came from the stalls. I saw the dance breaking up. The wake seemed far away, cut off as we were by the roar of rain.

And now our attention turned to the sight of people fleeing towards the hall. Martin and Barbara and Mistress Pyatt went by, crying out half-laughing about wet stockings and windswept hair.

No doubt Mistress Pyatt had been looking around for me and calling before she left. This was my moment to run out and follow her. I sensed that David expected me to go, but hoped I wouldn't. I hesitated a moment – then stayed still as they passed by.

Across the field the pig roast continued and men were still drinking. Ben Truelove ran past us, hand in hand with Alice, the youngest of the maids. I could not see Thomas Jevons, and guessed he had left in the direction of the road and the village, where his horse would no doubt be waiting.

The sound of rain on leaves created a soft enclosing roar in which David and I stood and looked at each other and smiled, not feeling the need for words.

But at last he sighed and said, "We should go back."
"Yes."

Lightning flashed nearby, startling us into action. He seized my hand and we ran, racing down the field, the last ones through the side gate, across the courtyard, into the shelter of the kitchen porch. We heard voices from inside, squeals of laughter. David took off his wet hat and shook drops from his hair. My cap dripped rain into my eyes and my own hair had come loose. We were breathless, laughing. He pulled me under the overhang, close against him. For this moment we were alone. I thought he would kiss me. I knew he wanted to. I saw it in his eyes. But then he broke away, pushed the door open, and drew me inside, into the warmth and noise. A boy came out of the kitchen in a blast of hot air and glanced briefly at us; on the stairs we heard footsteps hurrying down.

David let go of me, and wished me a formal goodnight.

Chapter Five

I was disappointed. We'd been so close, so eager. What had made him change his mind?

He'd sent me up the back stairs ahead of him so that we did not arrive on the top floor together, and now, as I hurried to the sewing room, I realised that Mistress Pyatt would be there and might well be angry with me.

"Mary? Is that you?" Her voice was sharp.

I went in. She had changed her gown, but her hair hung loose and damp.

"So you're back at last!" she exclaimed. "I was about to send John Frewen out to search for you."

"I was sheltering under—"

"Oh, I saw where you were! And no doubt the rain was a convenient excuse to stay there—"

Footsteps sounded in the passage outside, and we both heard David's door open. And close.

"Did Rob come?" I asked.

"No. And Meg went home early."

That was a reproach; one I deserved.

She tossed me a linen cloth. "Dry your hair."

I obeyed, squeezing out water, then fluffed my hair outwards to separate the strands.

She watched me in silence.

"We did nothing wrong," I ventured.

"Nothing wrong?" Anger burst out of her. "You stayed out there with Master Hawley when we all ran inside. And where *were* the two of you all afternoon? That witless little flibbertigibbet Nell came prancing up and told us all she'd seen you disappearing under the willows with the lady's secretary. Giggling, she was, and prattling away to me as if we were equals. How could you let me down like that, Mary? I thought I could trust you."

"I'm sorry." I saw now how I'd hurt her. She hated any familiarity from the maids. "We were down by the brook. Talking, that's all. And I picked some plants to draw…" I delved in my pocket and pulled out wet, crushed leaves, petals gone to mush. "We did not misbehave. Oh, but…" I thought of how abruptly we'd parted, and my voice wobbled as I said, "I do like him well."

She sighed then, and patted my hand. "Of course you do. I was young once myself."

I looked at her then, with her kind face and her faded brown hair falling around her shoulders, and saw her for the first time as a woman who had known love.

"You must miss your husband," I said.

"I did, for a long time. I'd known John Pyatt all my life and we were happy together. But I've been back here, a widow, for thirteen years, and my life is comfortable enough now."

"Do you have children?"

"None living. They all died as babies."

"All? That's sad."

"Only for those left on earth. They are with Our Lord now: Joan, Edmund and Cecily. I light candles for them and for my husband every time we make this room into a church. Father Taberer knows."

Father Taberer. There was something else I needed to ask. "Do you make confession to Father Taberer?"

Going to confession here at Lyde Hall was a thing I'd been worrying about, and putting off.

"Yes, of course," she said.

"I haven't – not yet."

I thought of the old priest, Father Barnes, who used to come now and then to our house in Dudley – always after dark, complaining of his aching bones in the cold weather. My brothers and I would tell him our childish faults. And he would pat Gilly and share supper with us.

Father Taberer, so learned and gentlemanly, was different.

"I don't know what to say," I admitted. "What sort of thing I should confess."

"You should say what is in your heart – on your conscience. Keep nothing back. It will unburden you."

The next day was a Sunday, but no Mass was said, either in the sewing room or in private chambers.

"Too great a risk," Master Bagnall told us when he called by in the morning. "One of the pursuivants was in the village yesterday, asking questions." He turned to me: "The lady wants to see you, Mary. She will send for you soon, so be ready."

He went downstairs, leaving me tense. I was in trouble now. I had danced with the pursuivant; I had hidden myself away with the lady's secretary. She would surely punish me.

Her summons came soon after.

"Tell her the truth." Mistress Pyatt said. "You've done no harm."

Oh, but I had! I should have ignored Thomas Jevons when he approached me. Refused to dance with him. Alerted John Frewen. I had put everyone in danger. I slipped downstairs and along the passage that led to Lady Chilton's parlour. A murmur of voices came from inside. I knocked softly.

"Come in."

She was with David and Father Taberer. David and I exchanged a glance, then looked quickly away, but I knew Father Taberer had noticed it. He was a worldly man who would miss little.

Trembling, I curtseyed to Lady Chilton.

"Mary," she said, "Master Bagnall tells me you met one of the pursuivants at the wake yesterday."

"Yes, my lady – the one who questioned me before." My voice came out high and anxious; my hands were shaking.

"Tell us what happened," said Father Taberer.

"I danced with him. I mean, he danced with me." I faltered, aware of David listening. "He was there when we changed partners, so I could not avoid him…"

"What did he say? Did he ask you anything?"

"No, Father. I got away from him quickly. But he'd remembered my name. And he told me *his* name."

"Which is?"

"Thomas Jevons. I remember something else now. He was talking to one of the grooms from the Hall: the youngest one, Ben. And Ben was shaking his head…"

I hoped fervently that I had not brought Ben Truelove

into trouble – but the incident had seemed strange. I was relieved when Father Taberer said, "Don't fear. Ben could not supply any information, even if he wanted to. He has already spoken to me about this."

But Lady Chilton frowned. "This Thomas Jevons surely does not live in the village. He came especially to the wake, and singled out our people. He may be looking for a weakness, trying the young ones first, those who can perhaps be frightened…"

"He won't frighten me," I said, then stopped, alarmed at my own forwardness.

But Lady Chilton said, "I believe you, Mary."

She had not mentioned my running around with David. Perhaps no one had told her. Father Taberer's glance at me was benign. David was looking down, holding his quill pen in one hand and smoothing its feathers between the thumb and fingers of the other.

I made a move to retreat.

"Mary – before you go…"

I looked up, heart thumping.

"Your work is excellent. The scarlet chasuble – very well repaired. I have been thinking about some new embroideries for the chapel. Of course I know we have no chapel at this time, only hidden places, but our hangings – the banners – are worn and faded, and I have a strong desire to renew them. I have seen some of your small designs. Would you feel able to undertake something larger?"

"Oh, yes!" I said. Relief coursed through me. "I should love to work on a banner."

I had never attempted such a thing, but felt sure I could do it.

She looked pleased. "A standing figure is always good for a vertical design. You have seen the banners we use for household Mass in the sewing room?"

I had. The two narrow banners were each hung from a bar. One showed the Virgin and Child, the other an angel blowing a faded gold trumpet.

"I will lend you my collection of patterns," she said, "and you may see if anything there takes your fancy. And you may have paper, and ink or charcoal, if you need it. Take your time, and show me your ideas when you are ready."

She made a small dismissive gesture; our discussion was over. But already I had inspiration: the figure on my banner would be a saint: a female saint, the one under the whitewash in our church at Dudley. I thought of the small foot showing beneath the chequered hem of her kirtle. I would re-create her in full; restore her to life in my embroidery.

As I turned to leave the room I caught David watching me. He gave me a discreet smile, and I knew he was pleased for me. If only we could meet and talk! Perhaps tomorrow...

But it didn't happen. At dinner times, during the next day or two, he sat as usual with the musicians, across the table from me, and seemed to be caught up in animated discussions with them. At other times he was at work, often closeted with Father Taberer and Lady Chilton and, sometimes, Francis Chilton. A gentleman visited them: a tall, dark man about the same age as Francis. Mistress Pyatt said he was Stephen Littleton of Holbeach House, which I knew was only a few miles south of Lyde Hall.

"Something's going on," said Kate Newey, when

I met her in the laundry room. "It'll be to do with the Jesuits, you can be sure."

She was washing a pile of fine linen ruffs and collars in hot water and soap jelly. The Chiltons' linen was too delicate for the lye and urine mixture in which we washed our sturdier linen at home.

"Will some priests be coming here, do you think?" I asked.

I remembered the excitement of that day when we'd hidden Father Taberer, and how it had brought us all together.

"Wouldn't surprise me," said Kate. "Whatever it is, you can be sure it'll mean extra work for us servants."

Kate was always at her happiest complaining – of fires that wouldn't light, collars with too many pleats, sheets with dog hairs on them. Small dramas erupted constantly around her.

"But it might be interesting," I ventured to say.

"Interesting always means more changes of linen," said Kate.

A few days later she was proved right. Master Bagnall called together all of us women servants, and we gathered in the sewing room to hear the news. He told us that visitors were expected any day now – a large number, including servants, nearly thirty people in all.

I felt, rather than heard, an in-drawing of breath around the room.

Master Bagnall, brimming with the responsibility of his role, said, "We shall need all the bedchambers swept and aired, and the bed hangings beaten. The rushes on the floors must be replaced, chimneys swept, sheets changed and the new ones aired and scented with lavender. Every room must be refreshed and made ready for use, even the smallest. New candles throughout. Windows to be cleaned, furniture polished with beeswax—"

"Is the King coming?"

Kate Newey always spoke out of turn. She was around forty, but as excitable as a child.

The steward looked at her in irritation. "No. Not the King. These visitors are gentlefolk, several of them ladies, and their servants. They are on a pilgrimage to St Winefride's shrine at Holywell in Wales" – now the intake of breath was audible, and there were murmurs of surprise or recognition, for we all knew of Holywell – "and staying along the way at several houses. We shall be honoured by their presence at Lyde Hall."

Inexperienced as I was, I knew we were not being told everything. If this were a pilgrimage of gentlefolk then surely there would be priests among the pilgrims? Such people usually sheltered a priest as a member of their family, as Lady Chilton did. I felt certain that some of the gentlemen would be priests travelling in disguise.

The preparations for the visitors began immediately, and Mistress Pyatt, as linen mistress, was responsible for making available sufficient linen for all the beds and ensuring that the best sheets were allocated to the better chambers. Two ladies were to have the spare bedchamber nearest Lady Chilton's, and several more of the party would sleep in chambers in the west wing, where Francis Chilton lived, and where there were some unused rooms. As I rarely saw my brother I was glad to be taken along by Mistress Pyatt and Master Bagnall on their inspection of these rooms. Rob himself had a tiny space – an annexe to his master's chamber, since he was expected to be available at all times. He was comfortably set up in this little room, with a bed, a large chest and hooks for his clothes, and a washstand. He was looking forward to the sudden arrival of so many grand visitors.

"Does your master know them all?" I asked.

"Oh, yes. Most of them. Or he knows of them. There will be plenty of talk and music. And a Mass, of course."

I lowered my voice. "Why didn't you come to the wake?"

He shrugged. "Busy."

"We expected you."

He knew I meant Meg, and looked somewhat ashamed. "Well" – he made a jest of it – "you must have got drenched, all of you."

Later, back in our own part of the house, Mistress Pyatt and I came upon Barbara, her arms full of linen, heading for the spare rooms that were kept for visiting priests. The doors – including the connecting doors between the rooms – all stood open, and Nell and Alice were in and out with brooms and wash cloths and pails of water. A sack full of old rushes stood in the doorway of David's room, ready to be thrown out. Two pallet beds were propped against the wall – for visitors' servants, I guessed. They would want their servants close at hand.

I saw the little grey cat crouching under the table outside the sewing room, awaiting her chance to dart in through one of the open doors.

"You'll be in trouble," I warned her.

From somewhere on the floor below I heard music – a viol – and someone singing: a man with a clear tenor voice – an angel's voice. It was church music, perhaps something for a Mass. The sounds broke off and I heard men talking, a phrase re-played; then the melody was picked up, and that voice, light but powerful, soared again.

"The musicians are practising," said Mistress Pyatt.

"Who is the singer?"

"I don't know. Probably Master Gale. He often sings. It will be good to have some music. I hope they'll perform some love songs and ballads as well – we all like those." She smiled. "You'll hear music throughout the house. We always have a little dance as we go about our work."

The visitors arrived a day later. Mistress Pyatt and I saw them approaching in the late afternoon – a golden afternoon such as we often have in early September. They came into view around the bend in the road, and we glimpsed them between the trees – men at the front and rear, and between them several ladies riding side-saddle with their skirts kilted up; the dark hood of a widow; servants riding behind with baggage. They rode without show, their horse trappings plain. And they carried no visible weapons, though I knew the men would be armed with swords under their cloaks, even on a pilgrimage – perhaps especially on a pilgrimage as they would undoubtedly be carrying offerings for the shrine: jewels and perhaps precious relics. They had come today from a great house near Worcester and were bound for Shrewsbury. They would stay with us two nights.

We opened the door to the passage, and met David emerging from his room.

"They are here, Master Hawley!" Mistress Pyatt said. "Come and see."

And he came into the sewing room and the three of

us leaned on the windowsill and watched as the party rode up to the door and John Frewen opened the gates. For a few moments David and I stood close together, our sleeves touching, listening as Mistress Pyatt commented on the people and their luggage and horses. But not a word passed between us.

Then from downstairs we heard an unaccustomed hum of voices and footsteps. I knew our people would be scurrying around, bringing wine and possets and platters of bread and meat, putting more logs on the fire, carrying out heavy cloaks and coats to be hung up and brushed.

"I must go down," said David.

I didn't want him to go. I'd hardly seen him since that day we'd come running in to shelter from the rain, and we'd not spoken once. I ached to be alone with him. Even to talk, now, with Mistress Pyatt here.

"Are they priests?" I asked him, "the men who will sleep up here?"

He hesitated – and I knew they were.

Mistress Pyatt intervened, reproving me. "Master Hawley is not at liberty to say, Mary."

"I – I know. I'm sorry."

I stood aside to let him go. But he brushed my hand – the merest touch – as he went by. Hope rose in me again, and a warm feeling of expectancy carried me through the rest of my afternoon's work.

Chapter Six

I was still mending bed linen and running errands around the house while the visitors settled in. Some of them were tired, and took supper in their rooms, while others could be heard in Lady Chilton's parlour below for much of the evening, talking together. Later I smelt incense and heard voices and music, and knew a Mass was being celebrated in the lady's private chambers.

Next morning, when Mistress Pyatt sent me down to the kitchen to fetch bread and small beer for the two of us, all was quiet in the rooms nearby. I thought the visitors were still asleep, but when I reached the ground floor I glimpsed through an open doorway several of them strolling and talking in the garden. Some were reading, some praying their rosaries. Father Taberer was there among them. And so was David, looking surprisingly at home in their company.

It was early. Dew glinted on wet leaves. Snail trails glistened, and a kitchen cat passed by, leaving dark paw prints on the damp path. I turned away reluctantly and entered the hot, busy kitchen.

Master Tandy looked up from pie-making and cast an irritable glance at me. "If you want anything today you must get it yourself."

As I poured beer into a pitcher, preparations for a feast went on around me. The kitchen smelt of baking bread. Honey dripped from a great comb in a bowl on the table. Baskets of windfall apples, of plums, and damsons, and currants both black and red, gleamed and oozed rich-coloured juice. Alice, her fingers stained purple, was sorting fruit, and Martin sniffed and wiped his eyes as he chopped onions.

Yesterday there had been a frenzy of plucking out in the yard, and the prepared ducks and geese were now laid in dishes along the table. Great sides of beef were already roasting over the fire, and little Ned Tolley was turning the spit. This morning several large carp had been taken from the fishpond and now lay on a board, dead-eyed, their bright scales fading.

Taking the pot of beer and a small loaf of bread, I left people to their work and went back upstairs.

"Master Bagnall came by," said Mistress Pyatt, "with instructions for the day."

"Already?" I set down the bread and beer.

"I think he started at the top of the house. There's to be dinner, of course, and everyone to be there. And later, Lady Chilton is to host a musical evening for our guests. Stephen Littleton will come over from Holbeach House. Oh, and her ladyship wants to see you."

"Why?"

"I don't know. But she will be at her morning prayers now and you are to see her afterwards."

I finished my drink, then washed and tidied myself

and smoothed my hair under a clean cap.

When we heard Father Taberer's voice in the passage I knew the lady's prayers must be over, and I hurried downstairs to her parlour.

Jane Shenton answered my knock. Apart from Jane, Lady Chilton was alone.

"Mary," she said, "you have heard that we are to host a gathering tonight – a musical evening?"

"Yes, my lady."

"I want you to be there, in the great chamber, to serve the gentlefolk and attend to their needs, especially the ladies. I shall be short of maids and you are far too comely to be wasted upstairs with nothing to do." She did not smile, but her gaze on me was amiable. I felt a glow of pleasure. I would see all the people in their finery and hear the music and singing. And I supposed – hoped – that David would be there.

"Now, what gowns did you bring with you from home?" Lady Chilton asked.

"I have the one I am wearing, and my good grey gown," I said.

"Then you will need something else. Come!"

She rose from her seat, enthused and energetic.

At the end of the room was a door into a small storage room full of the scent of herbs. They hung from the ceiling in dried bunches: lavender, rosemary, wormwood, meadowsweet and tansy.

There was a row of hooks on the wall with cloaks hanging from them in the shadowy, scented space. A great carved chest stood below. Jane opened the chest and brought out several gowns – all embroidered, all with contrasting laces – gowns that glowed with colour, even in this dim room. Was I to be allowed to wear one of these?

Lady Chilton signalled to Jane to lift and shake out a pale yellow gown, the colour of primroses, embroidered all down the front with flowers and foliage in green and rose.

"This was my daughter Anne's," she said. "Anne is much stouter now. Try it."

In no time I was undressed to my shift and laced into the yellow gown. Jane attached the matching sleeves with green laces.

"It looks well with your dark hair," she said.

I felt like a queen, but Lady Chilton said, "It's a little old-fashioned, but simple enough for a young girl. Take it to Mistress Pyatt; she will fit it to you."

Dismissed, I ran upstairs, carrying my own blue woollen gown.

Mistress Pyatt was unsurprised. "Her ladyship is generous," she said. "Now, stand still, while I see where to take it in."

At our midday dinner in the hall I did not wear the lady's gift, but brought out my own best gown, which was fine grey wool. I wore it with my green shoes, which always made me feel happy even though they pinched a little.

All the visitors were there, and I was able to look at them covertly, with quick glances. Although I knew several of them must be priests, it was often impossible to tell priest from gentleman. There were two couples, including a fair, handsome young gentleman with a pretty wife; and a tall dark man who I was sure was one of the priests since I had seen him in the garden with his breviary and rosary. Two of the ladies were apparently without husbands – one of them a thin, frail-looking but alert woman who ate sparingly and whose gaze rested often upon an older man. This man, I felt, was the power in the group, its leader; and I was sure he too was a priest. Lower down the table, among the servants, was a very small man – a dwarf, almost – whose appearance might have repelled me, only he had such a gentle air about him.

My brother sat within winking distance of Meg and me. Meg was made uncertain by Rob's attention; she looked pleased, but kept her gaze low. I frowned at him. He did not deserve to be forgiven easily. He appeared a little chastened but grinned at me, clearly determined that we should be friends again.

And David. He was across the board from us, between Henry and Ambrose. They were deep in conversation and he rarely looked up. I forced myself not to watch him. I did not want to seem bold – nor betray my feelings to others.

"Do you know any of the visitors?" I whispered to Mistress Pyatt.

"Some of them I've seen before," she said, her attention on a dish of savoury plums that was passing along the table. "The older man – I believe he's the leader of the Jesuits in England."

"Their leader?" I glanced at him again. A wanted man – and in this house. I felt an enjoyable shiver of excitement and danger.

"And the lady?" I asked.

I did not need to say which one.

"She is his protector – as Lady Chilton is Father Taberer's. She's a brave, devoted and outspoken woman, they say, not afraid of anyone, and well able to outwit the pursuivants."

"She looks unwell."

"I believe she is never very well." Mistress Pyatt had managed to secure the dish of plums and she spooned some onto her plate. "Will you have some of this?"

"A little." I wondered what sauce or spices were in the dish. At home we eat plain food.

"It may be for her health that they are undertaking this pilgrimage," said Mistress Pyatt.

In the late afternoon the gentry and visitors went to their rooms to rest, while I begged Mistress Pyatt's help to get ready for the evening.

Up in our tiny room I took off my everyday clothes and put on my best shift. This had ruffled lace at the neck and wrists and would show prettily beneath the yellow gown.

Mistress Pyatt helped me into the gown and smoothed the skirt.

"It's a much better fit now," I said. "Thank you."

She was pleased. "I have plenty of experience altering gowns."

She pulled the laces tight on the bodice and then helped me push my arms through the sleeves; these she tied in place with more laces at the shoulder.

I plaited my hair and we coiled the braids and fixed them at the back of my head. I wore my own cap – the best one, that I'd embroidered in a design of flowers and leaf tendrils.

Then we hurried along the passage to look at our work in the tilting mirror in the sewing room – and I saw myself transformed.

Mistress Pyatt smiled, and I turned and hugged her.

"You should come too!"

"Oh, I shall be lingering nearby – we always do on these occasions. Everyone likes to hear the music. But I'll be glad not to have to stand about in there."

Soon Stephen Littleton and his manservant arrived from Holbeach House, and with them a lean, flaxen-haired lad – a groom, I supposed – riding one horse and leading another pair.

We watched from our viewpoint in the sewing room, and saw Francis Chilton come out to greet the visitor and welcome him inside. Rob was there, a pace or two behind his master, and he helped the groom and manservant lead the five horses around to the stables.

I knew the kitchen folk would be busy again now, preparing a late supper to accompany the music; and down below I heard the musicians practising. There was no sign of David, but his absence only fired up my anticipation. I felt sure he would be there in the hall when the guests assembled.

Mistress Pyatt and I returned to our work. The sun was low and we needed to make the most of the remaining daylight before Lady Chilton sent for me.

But no sooner had we begun than Mistress Pyatt exclaimed that she had lost her pincushion. She sighed and stood up. "I must have left it in the bedchamber; I remember I took it with me when we were getting you dressed. Run and fetch it, will you?"

I darted out, along the passage and up the short run of steps that turned a corner at the top and led into our shared chamber.

I spotted the pincushion at once, lying on the chest, and picked it up and went out, closing the door. As I did so, I heard voices – one of them Francis Chilton's.

I peeped around the corner, reluctant to step out in front of a group of gentlemen. They stood at the top of the main staircase, at the point where the passage led on into the west wing where Francis had his private rooms. There were three men: Francis, Stephen Littleton of Holbeach House, and one of the pilgrims – the tall, fair young man. They were speaking in what seemed to me a low, urgent manner; and I saw how Francis, in particular, kept an eye on the staircase and glanced frequently up and down the passage, as if to ensure that they were not disturbed; and that, too, made me unwilling to show myself.

"…Horses," I heard Francis say. And Stephen Littleton said, "I shall be ready." I heard more mention of horses; and the young gentleman said something like, "The man… in London."

And then: several sets of footsteps, retreating along the passage towards the west wing; and silence.

I breathed again, and looked out.

No one was there, but I waited another few heartbeats before I moved cautiously down the steps into the passage.

I walked back to the sewing room slowly, the words I had overheard repeating themselves in my mind. Horses. Readiness. A man in London. What could they mean? Some transaction involving the purchase of horses, I supposed. The man must be a merchant. These noblemen were always buying horses – expensive horses – and talking about horses; for some of them, their lives revolved around the chase. Perhaps it was some secret deal. Certainly it was no concern of mine; but all the same I was glad I had stayed hidden. Something in their manner made me feel that all was not above board.

Soon I had forgotten the incident. It was time for me to join the company in the great chamber on the floor below. I could hear voices already, and the musicians were tuning up. I stepped cautiously downstairs, conscious of the yellow gown, the soft fullness of it under my hands – so different from my usual wear.

I slipped into the room at the lower end. Before this night I had only ever peeped in through the open doorway, since this was a private dining room where Lady Chilton and her son entertained friends or family. It was a room similar to the hall on the ground floor, though not as large, the walls hung with family portraits rather than armour and weapons. It contained a dining table, but this had been moved, and a smaller, more intimate space created at the far end, closed in by wood panelling and lit now by fire and candlelight that gleamed on goblets and glass and caught a glint of movement from the bows of the viols. The musicians were there, practising. Both Ambrose and Henry were playing, and someone was singing. I heard again that soaring voice – the one I'd thought to be like an angel's.

The singer was David.

He did not see me at first as I walked down the length of the room. He was singing in Latin – a song of joy, even rapture, it seemed, from its intensity – and I guessed it to be a song of praise to God. I was captivated by the beauty of his voice and the song, and knew I had lost my heart to him. Until that moment I had not put a name to my feelings, unwilling to call it love when nothing had been said between us. But now I was sure I loved him.

The song ended, and he looked across the room. The yellow gown had taken on a soft sheen in the candlelight and I saw how it surprised and delighted him and made him see me as if for the first time.

"Mary," he said, smiling as I approached. "I didn't expect you here tonight."

Ambrose and Henry stood up and greeted me.

"Lady Chilton wished me to wait on the company," I said. "But I fear I have come down too early." I felt embarrassed that in my anxiety not to be late I had ended up here alone among them.

But at that moment, to my relief, my brother bounced into the hall, and behind him came Barbara and Martin carrying wine and plates of food.

Rob exclaimed, "Mary! Where's all this finery come from?" And he came and grabbed me and swung me off my feet. "You look like a lady!"

"I'm here to serve the guests," I protested. And I felt my face turning pink and knew everyone there was looking at me. "Put me *down*, Rob!" I hissed.

He did, but kept an arm around me. "I'm here for the same reason," he whispered, "so you need not feel shy. The visitors will come in soon."

He too was dressed for the occasion in a fine doublet I hadn't seen before, and green hose.

Barbara and Martin set out the food and drink on the table. There were seed cakes, spiced beef, candied fruits, and a selection of Master Tandy's plum pies flavoured with different spices. I took note of everything since I would need to offer and serve it to the company.

The musicians now began to play one of those beautiful, familiar airs that people never tire of hearing.

David stood and listened this time as the guests entered in company with Lady Chilton and Francis and the two aunts, Lady Warne and Lady Vavasour. There was the tall, black-haired Stephen Littleton, the fair young man and his wife, the ladies and gentlemen. They all settled themselves around in the candlelit space, the ladies in full silk gowns with spreading skirts and the men in such grand and colourful breeches and doublets that no one would have guessed that several of them were priests in disguise. Lady Chilton was more animated than I had seen her before, and I realised how much she enjoyed company now that she had only her son at home – and he frequently away.

Rob and I moved unobtrusively among them, refilling glasses, handing around dishes of food, and providing anything else they needed. And all the time I was aware of David, and whenever I glanced at him I saw that he was looking at me.

Ambrose and Henry continued to play the sort of music that blends easily with conversation as the guests talked and ate. David sang to the accompaniment of Henry's lute, and as he sang and gazed at me I felt as if he were singing to me alone.

"Shall I go walk the wood so wild...
As I was once full sore beguiled...
My heart is like a stricken hind,
Alas! For love I die with woe..."

The feeling was so intense that I thought everyone must have noticed, and when the song ended and one of the ladies asked me for a herbal drink, I was glad of the opportunity to run down to the kitchen to fetch it.

There I found the maids and the kitchen folk at ease after their exertions – Martin and Barbara singing

Bonny Sweet Robin; Master Tandy humming along as he sat with a flagon of beer before him; and with them a flaxen-haired lad I recognised as Stephen Littleton's groom.

"Now, here's Mary looking like a fairy queen!" said Master Tandy – so I knew he'd been trying the wine before it was served. But he was sober enough to put out slices of fruit and sugared peel on a dish for me, and I took it, with the peppermint infusion, upstairs to the guest.

David was no longer singing when I came back in; he had sat down in a place partially out of my sight. I went to stand at the side of the room, watching and responding to requests, offering cushions to ladies who looked in need, and carrying plates of sweetmeats around from time to time.

The music had changed. Henry was now singing in Latin – something that sounded like part of a Mass. The chatter had subsided, and for the rest of the evening people listened. Some of the guests took part; and the older man – the one Mistress Pyatt had said was the leader of the English Jesuits – sang alone. He had a beautiful, mellow voice. David sang again the sacred song he had been practising when I came down to the great chamber.

I felt the emotion and belief and sense of shared suffering in the room. Some of these men, I knew, would have been in prison for long stretches of time, had perhaps even been tortured; and all of them who were priests had the threat of death hanging over them and must live as permanent fugitives in their own country. In the music they made together I felt both their joy and the burden it laid on them and the women who supported them.

Before it grew late Stephen Littleton took his leave, since he must ride home to Holbeach House.

The candles burned low. The sacred music continued. But soon the company began to stir and rise, with many thanks to Lady Chilton and Francis.

When they had all gone to their chambers, Lady Chilton came and thanked me, saying, "Go to your bed now, Mary. You have done well."

I looked across at the musicians and exchanged a brief glance with David. Then I left, leaving the young men to talk and snuff the candles.

Upstairs, Mistress Pyatt was hiding a yawn behind her hand.

"You're quiet this evening," she remarked.

"I'm tired," I said – though I was not. I had never felt more awake, more alive. But I wanted to be alone with my thoughts.

In bed in our tiny chamber Mistress Pyatt soon lapsed into her usual gentle snoring. But I lay awake, re-living the evening. I was uplifted, inspired – and on fire with love. I longed for David. I imagined him here with me now, our arms around each other, our breath mingling.

Later I heard men's voices in the passage nearby and the sound of doors opening and closing. One of the voices was his. The sounds quickly subsided and the last door closed. Beside me I felt the warm, unmoving bulk of Mistress Pyatt. Outside, an owl hooted, and the wind blew a spatter of rain against the window. I rearranged myself in the sliver of bed-space that was mine, and slept – never guessing what alarms and revelations the morning would bring.

Chapter Seven

It began peacefully enough at cock-crow: creaking floorboards, men moving about in the guest rooms across the passage, Mistress Pyatt murmuring as she clicked the beads on her rosary. I'm always sleepy in the mornings, and I rose unwillingly and splashed water on my face.

"Say your prayers," said Mistress Pyatt, as I yawned and sighed, struggling with the laces on my gown.

I obeyed her; knelt and asked God's blessing on the day ahead.

When we were both ready we went to the sewing room and began our day's work. An hour or two passed, and I stitched, absorbed in the embroidery on a fine linen shift that Lady Chilton had entrusted to me.

And then came urgent shouts: a warning.

Mistress Pyatt's hand flew to her heart. I heard footsteps, voices, on the stairs and along the passages. A door banged. Someone called out, "Turn the beds!" The clamour of voices made me shake with fear.

We hurried out into the passage and saw Father Taberer bounding up the last few steps to the top of the main staircase. Mistress Pyatt hurried to the back stairs and called to Barbara. David emerged from his room, along with the little stooped man I had seen in the great chamber at dinner time.

Father Taberer turned to David. "Are they hidden?"

"On their way up," said David. He glanced behind him, and I realised then that the fireplace in his room must be a false one that gave access to the attic hides.

Father Taberer nodded. "Good. But you, Brother Nicholas—?"

"I'll go into the stair hide," said the other man. He glanced at David. "The lad, too...?"

"No," said Father Taberer. "He's safe. He has a place here, like me."

I looked at David, and as our eyes met I was struck by a flash of understanding, as when a pattern lost in detail suddenly becomes clear. The realisation hit me with the force of a blow. *He has a place here, like me.* Like Father Taberer. I saw from David's face that I was right.

I wanted to fly at him, to demand to know more. But there was no time now to ask questions, or even to think.

Brother Nicholas had moved towards the hide in the grand staircase – the place where we'd hidden Father Taberer that time when he was almost caught at Mass. Brother Nicholas evidently knew the hide, for he opened it up at once and lifted out the tray that contained the velvet bag. He began to climb inside. Father Taberer helped him; and when the other man was safely down he closed the stair.

Now Barbara came hurrying along the passage. She turned to Father Taberer. "Lady Chilton says to tell you they are almost here. A small party, she says. Maybe nothing amiss, but best to be prepared."

"Thank you. I'll go down."

Father Taberer was dressed as a gentleman and would no doubt brazen it out as Lady Chilton's kinsman this time. As he went downstairs, Barbara said, "The lady wants you too, Master Hawley. And you, Mary."

But Mistress Pyatt, emerging from the priests' rooms, said, "Wait a moment. We must turn the beds."

"The beds?" I didn't understand.

While Barbara headed for the back stairs, Mistress Pyatt hustled me into David's room, which contained not only his curtained bed but also pallets on the floor. All had been slept in. In the adjoining rooms were more used beds. She told me to put a hand on one of the mattresses. "It feels warm, doesn't it? Anyone would know that someone had been in this bed – and not long ago. We have to turn them. All except David's."

David had followed us in.

"Brother Nicholas and I were on pallets," he said. "We can strip those and push them back under the bed."

We did that, and pulled the sheets and blankets off the other two beds and turned the mattresses over so that they felt cool and unused.

How Lady Chilton and the priests must rely on us all, I thought.

"We'll fold the bedding," said Mistress Pyatt, "and put it in the chest in the end chamber, so that all appears as usual. Now, Master Hawley, look around the rooms and make sure no one has left out anything that could betray them."

He shook his head. "I think these men are too experienced to leave anything. They carry almost nothing with them." There was awe and admiration in his voice.

Mistress Pyatt then declared herself satisfied, and told us to go down.

I could not look at David. Thoughts and memories were re-arranging themselves. His books. His room – here – in one of the chambers *known* as the priests' rooms. Seeing him walking in the garden with the priests yesterday. The way he withdrew from me after we fled indoors from the storm. *He has a place here, like me.* Like me. How could I have been such a fool? I had known from the start that this house was full of secrets. Why had I taken David for what he seemed?

But now I must put all these thoughts aside and help protect the priests. The two of us moved quickly to the back stairs. David gestured to me to go first, and I hurried down, anxious not to keep the lady waiting.

She was in her parlour. She had set up a scene, a tableau, ready for the arrival of the pursuivants. Jane sat behind her on a low stool. Seated around the room were some of the visitors: the fair-haired young man and his wife; another couple; a gentleman or two. Francis was there, and Father Taberer in his role as Lady Chilton's cousin, and the two aunts. There were small tables set with manchets, cold sliced meat and beer. Another table was set up for cards, and I saw piles of coin and hands of cards fanned out. Several of the ladies and gentlemen were playing, Father Taberer among them. In one corner of the room Ambrose sang softly and plucked his lute. David went to sit near him.

My brother stood near the far wall and signalled to me to come. I curtseyed to the company and went to join him, melting back against the wall. He took my hand and squeezed it as we heard voices and footsteps approaching.

"The game begins," he whispered, with a grin. But his hand was sweaty and I could feel the fear in him.

There came a discreet knock on the door: Master Bagnall. "They are here, my lady."

"Let them come in." Lady Chilton picked up her hand of cards and made a show of studying it.

The door opened wider, and they stepped inside: only two of them, so I knew there must be more downstairs and outside, looking around, asking questions.

The first in was an official-looking man dressed in a fine dark doublet with a high ruff and lace and a feathered hat that he swept off as he bowed to Lady Chilton. Rob whispered to me, "The sheriff's deputy."

Behind the sheriff's man was Thomas Jevons, whose eyes scanned the room and found mine. I tightened my hold on Rob's hand. From where I was standing I could no longer see David.

The lute fell silent.

"You have caught us at a late breakfast, sir," said Lady Chilton. "As you see, we have company. Will you join us in some refreshment?"

"We will not disturb your party, my lady," the sheriff's deputy said. "This is a courtesy visit only. There have been rumours of movements of men and horses in the area and we are checking on the safety of people in isolated houses."

"No doubt some of the movements of people were our visitors," said Francis. His words were civil, his voice cold. "You will know…" He introduced by name several people there who I supposed were from great houses in neighbouring counties.

The official bowed. I could see he was at a loss. There was no sign of any priest in the room, no evidence of Mass having been said. Only these grand people, at home, and at leisure.

"We believe Stephen Littleton of Holbeach House was here last night," he said.

"He is a neighbour," said Francis Chilton.

I thought suddenly of the horses: all the horses that must be in the stables. More than could be accounted for by the visitors gathered here. Perhaps it was not priests that the authorities were seeking after all. I remembered the conversation I had overheard at the top of the stairs.

"Some of the ladies are still in their rooms, resting, and taking breakfast," said Lady Chilton. "But if you wish to go further into the house..." She glanced at the far door. The two aunts, who I now realised had been placed strategically in front of it, shifted creakily in their chairs as if about to struggle to their feet.

"No, no. There is no need," said the deputy – and the aunts subsided. "We are not here to disturb anyone."

Had he really no idea that there were priests hidden in the attics? Wanted men; Jesuit leaders, from what I'd understood. Was he fooled or simply outwitted? Or looking for something different altogether? I glanced at Thomas Jevons and saw that he was watching Francis. I felt more than ever that it might be Francis who was under suspicion – but of what?

The two men bowed and left, and everyone in the room visibly relaxed. Ambrose began again to play and sing, and Lady Chilton signalled to me to come and offer food and drink to the guests.

"We will remain here for a while," she said, "in case

they return. But I think we may have got the better of them.”

“What about the horses?” I asked her – so concerned that I forgot it was not my place to speak. “There will be too many in the stables, won’t there?”

“The grooms had time to move some of them,” she said. “They will have taken them to the home farm.”

Francis spoke from beside the window. “They seem to be leaving – five men altogether. No doubt the other three have been looking around the grounds and stables.” His fists were clenched, his voice tight. “How long must we endure this surveillance – these restrictions on our liberty as Englishmen?”

No one replied, though there were nods and murmurs around the room.

At last Francis and Lady Chilton decided that it was safe to allow the priests out of their hiding places. She kept David with her, but Father Taberer and I left by the main staircase. Father Taberer went into David’s room and called up into the chimney space to the hidden priests, while I freed Brother Nicholas from the stair hide.

“You knew that hide,” I said to him – for he had a friendly manner and was easy to talk to. And I needed something – someone – to stop me thinking about David and who he really was. “Had you been in it before?”

Brother Nicholas smiled. “I designed and built it – along with many other hides, here and in other houses.”

“Oh!” I felt foolish, but he explained: “I’m a joiner by trade. These hides are my life’s work now – God’s work.”

We stepped up to the landing as he spoke.

“I’m servant to…well, I won’t name the priest. Been with him a good few years now. When we travel around I check on my hides and do repairs – and sometimes I’ll build a new one." A look of pleasure came into his face. "What I like most of all is a new house – or a new wing to a house. Then I can build a secret place into it right from the start. Those are the best hides."

"You must have saved many good men's lives," I said.

"I believe I have. I hope so."

"And now you go on to Wales? To St Winefride's Well?"

He smiled. "Blessed St Winefride, yes. All who come to her hope to find healing – of the body or the spirit. We travel in penitence and will walk the last mile barefoot. Do you know her story?"

"No," I said, "though I've heard of her shrine."

"Gwenfrewi was her real name," he said, sitting down on the step, and inviting me to join him, as if it were the most natural thing in the world to be telling a story while around us priests descended from the fake chimney in David's room, shook off dust, brushed cobwebs from their robes and chatted about their experiences. "She was a Welsh princess. Her uncle was Beuno, who also became a saint; he had built a church at the place that was later called Holywell. One day Caradoc, the son of a neighbouring lord, came visiting. He saw Gwenfrewi, and desired her, and wished to marry her. But Gwenfrewi had already chosen a different life for herself. She intended to become a nun. So she refused Caradoc. But Caradoc would not take no for an answer; he tried to force himself upon her, and she ran from him towards her uncle's church, crying out for help. The furious Caradoc drew his sword and struck off her head with one blow—"

"Oh!" I gasped. He had made the story so real I felt as if I had witnessed it.

"The head fell to the ground," said Brother Nicholas, "and Caradoc vanished, swallowed up by the earth, and was never seen again. St Beuno lifted his niece's severed head, and placed it upon her neck, praying all the time, and she was restored to life. Only a narrow white scar around her neck remained as witness to her martyrdom. But where the head had fallen a spring of clear water welled up, and in time a shrine was built around it, and it became a place of pilgrimage."

"And that is Holywell?" I said.

"It is: one of the greatest shrines in England, where people flock for healing, and cannot be kept away, even in these dark times."

"What happened to Winefride – Gwenfrewi – afterwards?"

"She became a nun, as she had always intended, and entered a convent at Gwytherin. In time she became abbess; and when she died she was buried there. She had her own path to follow, you see, and she stayed true to it – Ah! Now we must move from the stairs…"

We rose to our feet, and Brother Nicholas joined the priests and lay brothers who were going downstairs to meet up with the rest of their party. I did not have a chance to speak to him again.

There was no time for me to speak to David, either – not even after a Mass had been celebrated and the pilgrims had left and were on their way to Shropshire. David was downstairs all day – writing letters, or doing accounts, I supposed, for Lady Chilton, since he was employed as her secretary. But I now knew that these clerkly duties were a cover for his true profession. Throughout the afternoon I went over and over in my mind all my encounters with

David and saw them in a new light. Shame and anger built up in me, and I could not concentrate properly on my work. Once I pricked my finger and cried out in a temper; and Mistress Pyatt exclaimed, "Careful, now, Mary! Don't get blood on that linen!"

I was working on one of Lady Chilton's shifts, and I sucked my finger before a drop could fall and stain it. It's a sure sign of a novice to get bloodstains on your work. Experienced needlewomen don't prick their fingers, and I wanted to be seen as an expert. Tears sprang to my eyes.

"You're in a strange mood today," said Mistress Pyatt. "Is it time for your courses?"

I realised it was – but this reminder of my womanliness only made me feel more angry and miserable. Why had he deceived me? Why had he led me on? Or – even more bitter to think of – had I imagined his attention? I remembered the day of the wake, when we'd gone down to the stream and splashed around in the shallows, and talked about – oh, I don't know what: so many things, little things, that brought us close to one another. Surely I had not imagined his feelings that day? But there had been no hint of another meeting, no promise, no kiss. I longed to blurt out all my misery to Mistress Pyatt. I knew she would be kind. But I felt ashamed of having had such foolish hopes, of not seeing what was in front of my eyes.

"The light's going," I said. "And I'm tired."

I stabbed my needle into the pincushion and stood up.

At that moment I heard David's step in the passage, and then his door opening.

"Go down and see if the cooks have got something

tasty left over from last night," suggested Mistress Pyatt. "It'll do you good to move."

I went out into the passage, walked to the top of the back stairs, then stopped.

David must now be in his room, alone.

I crept back towards his door and knocked softly.

Footsteps inside made the floor creak. The door opened.

"Mary." His voice cracked.

I stepped over the threshold.

"Oh, Mary!" he said, and pulled me into his arms.

I pushed against him, fought him, gulping back tears. "Don't!" I exclaimed. "Don't. You're a priest. Why didn't you tell me you were a priest?"

Chapter Eight

He let go of me and closed the door behind us. I'd been watching his face and saw first shock, then relief.

"I'm not a priest," he said.

"Not…?" Could I have been mistaken? My hopes soared. "But…Father Taberer said…" I drew a hand across my face, smearing tears. "He said you had a place here, like him. And I remembered things you said and did…and I thought…"

He frowned, and paced about the room before turning to face me. "I'm not a priest. I'm not even old enough to be ordained. Not for several years. But I'm on my way to France – to Paris – to study with the Jesuits. They have a college there, and some – most – who study with them do become priests."

"So we can't… You *will* become a priest?" A celibate. I didn't say it, but the word hung in the air between us.

He nodded. "It's what I've wanted for a long time. What I thought I wanted…"

He reached out a hand to me, but I stepped away.

"Do they come back to England, these priests?"

"Yes. England is where they are needed. Most of them return to become part of the Jesuit mission."

"And that is treason." I said it on a whispered breath.

"I am no traitor, Mary, and never will be!" He looked appalled. "You must believe that."

"I do believe you. But to come back as a Jesuit priest – the law calls that treason. And I know what is done to those men when they are caught."

I gazed at him, at his strong young body, his beauty, his confidence. I saw him dragged on a hurdle to the place of execution, his face bruised and beaten, his hair matted with blood and dirt. I tried to shut my mind to imagining more. I had never witnessed it, for which I thanked God, but I knew it, every detail. The great fire in front of the gallows; the brief hanging, before the man was left alive to experience what followed: the male parts sliced off and tossed into the flames; the belly slit to spill the guts; everything thrown on the fire before the victim was taken down, decapitated and hacked into four pieces. The stench, the blood, the screams, the heat, the roar of the crowd.

"I can't bear it," I said. "I can't." My eyes flooded with tears, and I felt his arms go round me, his face close, his breath mingling with mine.

"Don't fear what may never happen," he said.

"Don't *you* fear it?"

"It is martyrdom. Glorious, not to be feared."

"*Glorious?*" I pulled away and stared at him in horror.

"Mary," he said, "I am not yet a priest. I may never be one. I am unworthy of martyrdom. I'm going away to study. That's all."

"But – when? When will you go? And why are you here, at Lyde Hall?"

"I'm waiting for a passage to France. We will travel secretly, in a small group. It's dangerous. The authorities are on the watch for groups of young men like me. We are hidden in Catholic houses until it's safe for us to move on. A ship must be found, and a trustworthy captain; and then we must wait for the tide. We sail from Gravesend, but it's better not to wait there. All the time there's the risk of being caught and arrested."

"How will you know when to go?" There was a hollow feeling inside me. He was leaving. Soon. I would lose him.

"Someone will come for me – an escort. I expect a message any time. Then they may move me to another safe house, or we may travel immediately to Gravesend under some disguise." He shook his head and gave a great sigh. "It's hard, this waiting. I thought I would be on my way before now. I – I didn't anticipate...you."

I said bitterly, "And now you wish you *were* gone, and rid of me."

"No! No, I don't. Only – oh, I want *everything*! To go, and to stay..."

"Why didn't you tell me? Why did you lie to me and let me believe you were Lady Chilton's secretary?"

"I didn't lie."

"You didn't tell the truth."

"I was warned when I came here not to tell anyone who didn't need to know. Father Taberer and the lady arranged for me to come. She truly was in need of a clerk; that was known, so no one was surprised. I think Henry and Ambrose may suspect. But no one else knows. I felt sure I should not tell you."

"So you let me believe you were free to..."

"I did, and I'm sorry for it. I've been in such delight and anguish over you. I didn't know what to do – how to stop…"

His arms went around me then; and this time I didn't push him away, but moved closer. He lowered his head to mine, his lips brushing my cheek. Our noses bumped together; we shared a breath, a gasp; and in a moment we were kissing each other as if it were the most right and natural thing in the world. And I was lost. I could not give him up. I would fight to keep him.

A footstep in the passage outside made us spring apart. I stared at him: he was bright-eyed, flushed, untidy. My hands flew to my hair, tucking in ends, and I cast about for a mirror – but there was none. My heart was pounding, and I knew my face would be blotchy; it always is when I cry.

Whoever it was passed by, and we relaxed and breathed, came close again.

"We can't—"

"No…"

But I knew we would.

Not now. This moment had gone. I remembered Mistress Pyatt, who had suggested I run down to the kitchen – how long ago? I'd have to say I'd been kept talking. She'd believe me. She'd seen that I was upset about something.

He stepped cautiously to the door, listened, and opened it.

"Go now," he whispered, kissing my ear as I slipped past him into the passage. I walked down the stairs to the kitchen, more slowly than usual, trying to calm myself. I'd bring back some sweet thing from the feast for Mistress Pyatt, I thought, and hope it took her mind off me.

That night I could not sleep for excitement and guilt. What were we to do now? How were we to meet? He was so near – only a few steps across the passage – and yet out of reach. I could not be seen to go there – could only hope for chance meetings.

During the week or so that followed we met most days at dinner time, entering or leaving the hall, and sometimes his hand briefly caught mine. We listened for each other and met as if by chance on the bend of the stairs or in the passageways around the kitchen and courtyard, where we snatched quick kisses. The cat, slipping from one room to another, gave us excuses to stop and talk and touch hands. In most of these encounters there was no time for more than a brief word or glance. I had to force myself not to look at him, not to talk about him. I avoided the maids and their chatter and instead sought Meg's company. She asked no questions, but she must have noticed the change in me. My greatest fear was that Lady Chilton would notice, or that someone – Jane? – would tell her. In a house like this everyone was trained to be watchful. But Lady Chilton seemed unaware; she was pleased with me.

Although I was so caught up in my excitement over David, rather than interfering with my work this feeling released in me new energy and ideas. Lady Chilton had asked me for a design for a banner and, now that the visitors were gone, I found inspiration. My idea had been to recreate the saint hidden under whitewash in the Dudley church. I saw now that this saint must be St Winefride. Ever since I'd heard her story from Brother Nicholas I had felt it had meaning for me, and I came to believe that these two saints were truly one and the same. I would portray St Winefride with a fine scar around her neck, and at her feet the miraculous spring of water bubbling up from the green turf. In the background would be St Beuno and his church. The colours would be watery: green, blue, and silver, with touches of russet and gold for richness. There would be a border of water plants with twining stems, like those I had found by the Lyde brook on the day of the village wake.

I went out to the garden and around the house, looking at plants, at pictures of saints and at old banners and hangings. On one of these explorations David contrived to meet me in a little-used passageway. We kissed and clung together, but I felt that he was unhappy.

"What can we do?" he whispered. "This never gets any easier. There is no way, except…" But then he caught me to him and held me even closer.

When Lady Chilton sent for me a day or two later I was sure she must have found me out. I would be dismissed. David would be barred from the priesthood. But she only wanted to hear my ideas for the banner. Words tumbled out of me as I talked to cover my shock. She was greatly pleased with everything I proposed.

"A St Winefride banner would honour not only the saint," she said, "but our friends and priests who stayed here on their way to her shrine. Your ideas are excellent, Mary. Now, if you need paper, drawing materials…"

"I will, my lady."

"Then Master Hawley will bring them to you. He looks after such things for me."

*

David came to the sewing room later that day, bringing a few precious sheets of paper, a slate, charcoal, chalk, ink and a quill.

"Paper and ink!" Mistress Pyatt was impressed. "The lady must value your work, Mary."

"She does," said David. He murmured that there was more paper if I needed it. He looked ill at ease. It's because Mistress Pyatt is here, I thought.

He left us then; and it was only when I came to gather and sort the sheets of paper that I found the letter he had hidden between them: a small folded square, sealed with wax and addressed to me. I slipped it quickly into the pocket under my gown. I was desperate to read it. But when? Where?

Mistress Pyatt and I continued our work till it was time for supper. I sketched, and thought, and rubbed out, and sketched again, till the slate was dusty. And I kept touching my skirt, where my pocket was, and feeling the stiff shape of the letter waiting for me.

At last I broke off early and exclaimed, "I need some air! I'll go for a walk in the orchard and fetch our supper from the kitchen on the way back."

I knew Mistress Pyatt would not want to join me in a walk.

I hurried downstairs, along the kitchen passage and out into the grounds. The orchard lay beyond the stable block. At this hour, with the light fading and long shadows on the grass, it was growing cool. No one else was there, though many of the later-ripening trees had apples ready to fall. I walked to the bottom of the orchard and hid myself away, sitting on an abandoned wooden crate that lay against the wall.

My hands trembled as I broke the seal. A letter seemed such a solemn, important thing that I feared it must be bad news: perhaps that he was to leave tonight for Kent.

But when I unfolded it I saw that it was surely too long for that. The script was clear enough, but I am no scholar and it took me a while to read and take in what he said.

"*Most dear Mary,*" he wrote.

Forgive me if this letter hurts you. I have been at work on it, writing, striking out, rewriting, pacing up and down my room – at night, when I should have been thinking of my sins and asking forgiveness of God. It is some time since I went to confession, and I know I should go again – for the fault is all mine. I am older than you, and a man, and ought therefore to have had the more judgment and wisdom.

You know I am committed to a life of prayer and study, and to travelling to Paris, to the college there. My parents are like yours: they are Catholics but conform to the Protestant church; if they did not my father would be unable to pursue his profession. I used to talk to the priests who came secretly to our house and learned about their lives and admired them. When I left school my father set me up with an apprenticeship to a cloth merchant in the centre of town. The work interested me and introduced me to many people I would not otherwise have met – among them some recusants. This summer I completed my apprenticeship – but already

I had begun to feel a yearning for something more. I have always been inclined towards the spiritual life, and last year an old school friend introduced me to Father Taberer, who was travelling at that time in disguise. It was Father Taberer who guided and instructed me, encouraged me in my singing, took me under his wing and introduced me to other like-minded men. And of course it was he who found me this safe house here at Lyde Hall.

Always, when I meet with the Jesuits, I feel at home. You remember the priests who came with the pilgrimage? They had such certainty – such joy. One of them – I must not say names – one of them in particular made me laugh with his stories: the narrow escapes he had, the adventures, the disguises. He suffered grievously in prison and yet never wavered. And he brought many people to reconciliation.

Mary, I am bound by my choice, and I should never have let you – or myself – believe otherwise. We must not think of each other, though it breaks my heart to say it. You must turn your back on me, and I will endeavour to do the same, dear Mary, though I love you and always will.

D. H.

Beneath his initials he had written: *"Burn this. We are warned not to write letters."*

I crumpled the letter in my fist. I *was* hurt, and angry – with David, and also with Father Taberer. Although, if it wasn't for Father Taberer, I now realised,

I would never have met David. And those priests on the pilgrimage: I remembered how David had kept away from me after they left. I had been fired with love for him at the very time that he was being filled with renewed belief in the Jesuit mission. But was David truly so sure that he knew his own mind? Or was he influenced by the priests?

I smoothed the sheet of paper out, re-read it. Would he ignore me from now on? Did he expect me to do the same? How could I? I could not let him go. I would fight for him.

I did not get a chance to speak to him the next day, and I felt he was avoiding my eye. It made me all the more determined to seek him out.

That night, when Mistress Pyatt and I were on our way to bed at our usual time, I noticed a faint glow of light showing under the closed door of David's chamber.

"Master Hawley's studying late again," she murmured as we walked on up the passage.

We climbed the steps to our own room and she began preparing for bed. I went to the window and looked out. I'd been talking to Rob earlier, and he had told me there was to be an eclipse of the moon tonight. These partial eclipses of the moon are common and often hidden by cloud, but they always give me a slight shivery feeling. And this one, Rob had said, was to be followed in two weeks' time by a much rarer event – an eclipse of the sun. He'd been in a strange mood: intense, excited.

From our small window I could see only cloud. But the night before, if you craned your neck, the moon had been visible.

"Aren't you coming to bed?"

Mistress Pyatt was already in her shift, but I had not even begun to undress.

I told her about the eclipse.

"Oh." She yawned. "I've seen enough of those in my time. People say they mean something but, if they do, watching won't change it. Blow the candle out when you get in."

She was soon asleep.

I looked out; saw the moon sail free from streamers of cloud. A shadow that was not a cloud nudged its rim.

It's beginning, I thought. And in my heightened state of awareness it seemed to me that the eclipse must be a sign, a warning.

But I had not stayed up to look at the moon. What I saw in my mind was that thin line of light under David Hawley's door.

I did not blow out the candle. Instead I took it with me as I opened my own door and slipped out. I trod cautiously on the steps, following their curve down into the passage. A faint light came from the leaded window above the main stairs, but it was a dark night, and would grow darker.

The light still showed under David's door. When I knocked he opened it immediately, as if he knew it must be me, and drew me in. He was still dressed, but without a doublet, and I felt the warmth of his body through his linen shirt as he embraced me.

"Mary, you should not have come here," he whispered. "If anyone saw you, your reputation would be lost."

"I don't care," I said.

"But you should care. You must not risk your good

name for me. I'm not worth it. Did you read my letter?"

"Yes."

"And you've burnt it?"

"Yes." I had, all except the last line and his initials, which I'd torn off and hidden in my needle case.

He glanced at the table under the window, where his candle stood, and I saw loose pages of writing.

"More letters?" I said.

"I'm trying to write to my parents, to say farewell." His eyes looked tired, red-rimmed, with a sheen of unshed tears. "It's so hard. My mother..." The tears overflowed and rolled down his face. "She will miss me unbearably."

I reached out to comfort him, but did not know how. And for the first time I thought of that other woman's suffering. She too was losing him, perhaps never to see him again.

He regained control. "Father Taberer says he can arrange for its safe delivery when the time comes."

"So you *will* go? And soon?" I put all shame aside and begged him, "Don't go! Don't become a priest. Stay with me. I love you."

He groaned, and put his arms around me and held me fiercely. "And I love you, Mary. I feel so torn. I've worked for years towards this. It was always my longing to go to France and study – and, if I was able, to become a priest. Father Taberer has been teaching me. He has arranged everything. Only now" – his voice broke – "you've made me question my fitness for the priesthood, my commitment. I thought I knew what I wanted, but it's so hard to give you up."

"Then don't." I could feel his heartbeat.

"I must. And you will find someone better – someone worthy of your love."

He moved, still with his arms around me, towards the door. "Go now," he said, almost thrusting me out. "You must not be caught here. And I must write this letter. You *must* go. Please."

Chapter Nine

"Bless me, Father, for I have sinned."

The blessing, in Latin, came from behind the curtain – a linen sheet, thin with age, hanging from a rail in a spare first floor chamber. The curtain was a formality, since everyone knew the priest was Father Taberer, but I was glad of the privacy it provided. I was sure I would not be able to speak if we were looking at each other.

I had to start with easier sins. This was my first confession at Lyde Hall. When I arrived I had been told I could go to confession whenever I wished; but no one had insisted upon it, and I had felt nervous, unsure of what to say, and kept putting it off, week by week. How I wished now that I had not left it so long! Back in August I had only minor sins, but now it seemed that I carried a great burden.

I drew breath. "I have spent time on dress, on vanity – time I should have given to prayer. I boasted to Mistress Newey about my embroidery skills; I have too much pride in my work…"

"Pride in one's work can be a good thing," Father Taberer murmured, encouragingly. He knew there was more.

I took a breath. "I have thoughts about a young man. Thoughts a maiden should not have."

"A particular young man?"

"Yes," I whispered. "One who – who is not free to marry me."

"Thoughts?"

This was so hard. "And kisses; tears."

Haltingly, in a low voice, I confessed all our meetings and contrivances, and my part in leading David into sin.

"Dominus noster Jesus Christus te absolvat…ego te absolve a peccatis tuis in nomine Patris, et Filii, et Spiritus Sancti. Amen."

The absolution. I knelt on the floorboards, the makeshift curtain swaying softly as Father Taberer moved and breathed behind it. I had made an act of contrition and had received a penance – a series of prayers to repeat that would absorb my time and subdue my desires.

I felt cleansed. As I left, I made a promise to myself that I would give up all desire for David. I thought of Eve, and how she tempted Adam and they were both cast out of the Garden of Eden. Eve was the cause. Women were innately sinful. I knew this. David was destined for the priesthood, for a celibate life, and I must give him up.

And I tried hard to do so. I prayed. I worked at my embroidery. I kept away from his room.

But we saw each other constantly. It was impossible not to meet, at dinner and around the house. And when we met we talked, if only in brief whispers.

"I've been to confession."

"So have I."

"I thought it would help," I said, "but nothing has changed, has it?"

And, despite his look of strain and tiredness, I felt a leap of joy when he said, "No," and I knew I had not yet lost him.

Less than a week after I'd been to confession, near the end of September, Lady Chilton sent for me to come and sit with her, bringing my embroidery.

Although the message did not sound threatening, I felt anxious. Lady Chilton must by now have seen what was going on between me and her secretary, and the strain it was causing us. And even if she hadn't, someone else might have told her. Not Father Taberer; the seal of the confessional would prevent that. But Jane...the aunts... And Lady Chilton knew the truth about David and would want his transfer to France to go smoothly.

I had now begun work on the St Winefride banner, so I took that with me.

Lady Chilton was in her parlour, with her own embroidery set up on a frame in front of her. To my surprise, no one else was there, not even Jane. This made me even more uneasy. The lady's focus was all on me. I noticed that she looked pale and her eyes were dark-shadowed, unlike her usual robust appearance.

I curtseyed, lowering my gaze.

"Ah, Mary," she said. "Come in. How is the design progressing? Let me see your work."

I knelt beside her and unrolled the cloth so that she could see what I'd been working on. I had begun by outlining the figures and setting the border pattern. We spent some time talking about my plans and the colours, and my anxiety gradually disappeared as I realised I had her approval.

"Bring a stool," she said, "and sit near me, and we will work together."

As I settled myself she said, "You are an asset to this house, Mary. I was talking about you with Lady Warne, and she is of the same mind. Your designs and your stitching are a gift from God that you must endeavour to use for His glory. Mistress Pyatt always speaks well of you. We all find you a most capable and willing girl, and I am glad to have you in my service."

I bowed my head modestly. "Thank you, my lady." What more was coming? Was there a 'but'? I guessed I was not here simply to show her my work, nor keep her company, and I waited nervously for some words of chastisement about David. To my surprise they did not come.

"Next week," she said, "next Sunday, we will celebrate Michaelmas."

I looked up, startled.

"You had forgotten? Well, you are a town girl." She smiled. "I thought you might like to go home for the holiday. Your brother can take you. My son has given him leave to go home for a few days. It's time you saw your family. You will have missed them, no doubt?"

"Yes," I said – though in truth I had scarcely thought of my family these last few weeks. But I recovered my manners and managed to say, "Thank you, my lady," while thinking: I don't want to go! Don't send me away – not now. Don't separate me from David. Suppose his contact arrives and takes him while I am gone? I won't be able to bear it.

But if she knew what she was doing to me, she gave no sign.

"I will ask Master Tandy to send some sweetmeats with you for the feast," she continued amiably. "You will have a goose, I suppose?"

"Yes," I said. "We always have a goose at Michaelmas. And my mother will be glad to see all her children together."

"That's settled, then. You shall go home for Michaelmas, and perhaps again at All Souls, and of course Christmas."

"Thank you, my lady."

I bent my head to my work. I knew there must be more. She did not need me here sewing with her, and Jane absent, simply to give me leave to go home.

We stitched in silence for some time. And then she said, "Does your brother have any worries, do you think?"

At once a whole flock of uneasy thoughts flew into my head. About Rob and his master: where they went, who they knew, what they were involved in. But how could I explain such vague anxieties to Lady Chilton? I said, "I don't know, my lady. I rarely see him. But I believe he is well."

"He does not confide in you?"

"No."

She hesitated, then said, "I am concerned about my son. He seems…busy, nervous, preoccupied. He rarely tells me what he is involved in, or where he is going. Well, why should he? He has long since come of age. But he is a man of principle and proud temperament, and these are difficult times for Catholics. I sometimes fear... He keeps your brother close, and perhaps in his confidence?"

As she spoke I had been remembering things: Rob's sweaty hand holding mine when the sheriff's man had come to the house, and Francis's furious outburst afterwards. But none of that had been surprising; Francis was naturally angry at the intrusion into our gathering – and probably fearful, too, since we had several priests hidden in the house.

I remembered the conversation I had overheard on the stairs. Little had been said, though its tone had made me uneasy. But how could I explain that to Lady Chilton? It might seem as if I'd been eavesdropping. And I could not even remember it clearly now. Something about buying horses. A man who was ready. Some business transaction, and surely no concern of mine, or hers.

But Lady Chilton knew her son well. If she too had become suspicious, perhaps it was with good reason.

The truth was that I didn't like Francis Chilton. I thought him a cold, arrogant man. He treated Rob well, and he kept him in fine clothes because Rob's appearance reflected his master's own standing. The household servants, on the other hand, especially we women, were beneath his notice. And he would snap his fingers at Master Bagnall the steward to gain the man's attention, or dismiss the musicians with an abrupt "Enough!" But none of this meant that Francis could not be trusted or was a danger to Lyde Hall – or to Rob.

"You are quiet, Mary," said Lady Chilton. "Is there something...?"

"My brother does not share anything important with me," I said. "I'm just his little sister."

"Well" – she attempted a smile – "you will enjoy a visit home with him, will you not?"

"Yes, I will. Thank you, my lady." I wished it were true.

She looked at me keenly, and in silence. Then she said, "You may be just Robert Wilshaw's little sister, but I think you already know some of the secrets of this house and its people. You know, for instance, that my secretary is not all that he seems?"

"Yes." I could not meet her eye.

"David Hawley will soon be on his way to Paris," she continued. "He is unlikely ever to return to Lyde Hall."

"I know." It came out as a whisper.

"According to Father Taberer, David is an intelligent, dedicated young man of great promise whose longing is to serve God and bring the true faith back to England." She leaned towards me. "England has great need of such people: men of learning, courage and belief, young and strong enough to survive the rigours of a priest's life in these dark times."

I raised my eyes to hers. I could not speak.

"You must let him go, Mary."

Chapter Ten

It was risky going to David's room, but that was the only place where we could meet without fear of being seen. The lower floors of the house were busier with people; in the garden we always felt the many windows overlooking it to be full of eyes; and after Lady Chilton's warning I dared not be seen talking to him in public, even briefly.

As we left the hall after dinner the following day I caught his eye and he gave the briefest of nods. I waited a moment, then detached myself from the other women and climbed swiftly upstairs.

He heard my footsteps, opened the door, and I slipped into the room and into his arms. For several moments we kissed and clung together, and all I could think about was our closeness, the press of his body against mine. My arms tightened around him, and I thought: I will never give him up, never.

When at last we broke apart, I whispered, "Lady Chilton knows. She was not angry. But she said I must stay away from you."

He nodded. "And Father Taberer – well, he won't

breach the secrets of the confessional and name names, but he warned me about lust and the wiles of women."

Father Taberer again. I felt desperate.

"I'm going home for Michaelmas," I said. "For several days. Promise me you won't leave for Paris before I come back. Promise!"

"They won't come for me during Michaelmas."

"But if they *do*..."

"They won't. They'd send a message first, several days or a week beforehand, to warn me to be ready. And – well, I'm not prepared, spiritually. I've told Father Taberer I feel unsure, unworthy even to think of becoming a priest."

I felt a lift of the heart – which was cruel of me, for I saw how tormented he was.

"What did he say to that?" I asked.

"Oh, he says I have nothing to worry about, that I have taken no vows yet; I am simply going to study at the college. I'll have time, he says – as much time as I need."

"But he wants to get you there, to this place in Paris?"

Father Taberer saw me as the enemy – that was clear.

"Yes." His eyes lit and he smiled. "He says I will love Paris; that it's a beautiful city; and I will meet others like me, and we will study and talk and read..."

I glanced at the book that lay open on his table. It was in Latin. He'd shown it to me before, so I knew it was *The Spiritual Exercises* of St Ignatius of Loyola. Beside it, also open, lay David's journal, full of notes in his neat, clerk's handwriting.

I will lose him, for sure, if he goes to Paris, I thought.

He must have seen that fear in my face, for he reached out and held me close. "Everything feels right and natural when I'm with you," he said. "Perhaps God sent you to show me that I am unsuited to the life of a priest."

"Perhaps he sent me to make you happy and give you a life such as other men have," I retorted. It was bold of me, but his words, with their suggestion that I was merely an instrument, had stung. I was more than a temptation sent to snare him. I was Mary Wilshaw, who loved him and would wait for him.

He said, "If we—" But then came quick footsteps in the passage and a knock on the door.

We sprang apart. My heart was hammering.

"David?" Henry Gale's voice, light and cheerful as always.

I fled into the adjoining room and hid myself behind the bed curtains.

I heard Henry come in, and the two men greeting each other. They spoke together for several minutes about some music for the lady's private Mass that evening. Standing behind the hangings, trying not to move or breathe in the dust from the curtain folds, I heard their voices, paper rustling, a snatch of song from Henry; then David picking up the tune, uncertain at first; brief laughter; another try, more confident this time. They chatted; laughed.

How long would Henry stay? Could I escape through another door? I longed to move, to be free of the fear of discovery.

At last, to my huge relief, I heard the voices rise in farewell. Henry was leaving; the door opened and closed; his footsteps passed my room and faded towards the back stairs.

I stepped out from behind the curtain as David came into the room.

"Mary, I'm so sorry..." He tried to put his arms around me, but I stiffened; I could not respond to him. I felt shamed and frightened.

"I must go – now," I said.

"Don't fear. Henry won't—"

"Please. Let me go."

And so we parted, with unease between us, and I did not get another chance to speak to him before I went home for Michaelmas.

Rob and I left Lyde Hall on Saturday, the day before the feast day. I rode pillion behind him as we set off across country to pick up the Dudley road. The woodland tracks are often muddy, but we'd had fine weather and it was mostly dry underfoot, with drifts of yellow leaves. The chase was full of the golden light of late September. After a while we both dismounted and walked, leading the horse, which was laden with our baggage. We brought spare clothes and a basket of gifts from Lyde Hall for the feast: cured meat, pears, apples, bunches of herbs, a stoppered jug of wine, and some of Master Tandy's pastries.

I'd felt so low after my last encounter with David that I scarcely cared what clothes I packed, but Mistress Pyatt had insisted that I take the yellow gown to show my mother, so it was there, folded carefully, along with two fine linen shirts of Rob's.

We'd have made rich pickings for robbers on the road, but we wore our everyday clothes and Rob carried a dagger in his belt, and we encountered no one but a woodcutter on his way to Sedgley, and some charcoal burners. We heard voices and the sounds of axes and shovels, and came out into a clearing where plumes of smoke rose from charcoal mounds. The men at work there looked up as we passed; eyes flashed white in blackened faces. Across the clearing were the wooden booths where they lived all summer. Soon all these men would be gone, their booths left empty, but the warm days held them here for now.

At first I kept thinking of David – the way we'd parted, what must have seemed like my coldness towards him, and the fear that he'd be gone before I returned. To my relief, Rob didn't notice. I'd expected him to be asking, "What's up, our wench?" and teasing me, but he too seemed distracted. Unlike me, he was alert, excited, whistling a snatch of tune – some jaunty soldiers' song – his hand straying unconsciously to his dagger. Once or twice he asked me if I wanted to ride, but I said no – I felt freer walking. We picked late blackberries and ate them, spitting out the pips as we walked. And I gathered oddments from the forest: an acorn cup, oak leaves, grasses heavy with seed-heads. At home I'd lay them out and draw them for embroidery ideas. That was a pleasure to come. My heart began to lift in spite of everything.

Once on the Dudley road we re-mounted, and soon we saw the great round tower of the castle rising above the town, and the road began to fill up with horses and wagons and people on foot. We were all slowed down by a flock of geese walking ahead of us in the road, driven by a barefoot girl in a patched gown. A great clamour rose from the birds, and green goose-shit spattered the road; you could see that several flocks must have passed along here in recent days. We rode slowly behind them all the way into the town. It was a market day and the centre was full of booths and traders and penned animals.

Our family home – the house and shop – is only a few minutes' walk from the crowded market square, in one of the quieter streets nearby. It has a long frontage, with a workplace and a shop on the ground floor and living space upstairs. At the side is an arched entrance through which we led the horse into a yard and stable. It all seemed small to me after being at Lyde Hall for so long; and there was no groom to run and take the horse from us and brush him down. Rob was unstrapping the saddlebags when the back door opened and our mother hurried out.

"Mary! Rob! Oh, it's good to see you both!"

She threw her arms around me. "You look well, Mary, but" – she looked intently at me – "a mite…tired? Is that it? Are you sitting too long at your needle? I hope they allow you fresh air?"

"They do, Mum," I assured her – and was saved from further enquiry by Rob, who came to join us in a three-fold hug.

"Come in, come," she said, and I fetched the basket of gifts from Lyde Hall and went in ahead while Rob picked up the saddlebags.

There was a good smell of cooking: pottage, I guessed, and perhaps some fish, since Saturdays are fast days. Tomorrow was the feast of St Michael the Arch-angel, which we would celebrate as Catholics, quietly, in our own home, before attending church.

Rob set down the bags in the passage, and my mother and I took the basket into the kitchen, where Joyce was checking dishes and young Bess stirring something over the fire. Both left their work to come and greet me and exclaim over Master Tandy's pastries and the fragrant herbs.

"We'll have a feast tomorrow," Joyce told me. "There's a goose on the cold slab out back, and herbs and vegetables from the garden, and an apple pie." She turned to Bess, her voice sharp. "Watch that sauce, bab! Don't let it catch."

"Why don't you go and rest, Mary," my mother said. "Rob's taken your bag up. I'll call you when dinner's ready."

I went upstairs, passing the door to the parlour, where we'd soon be assembling, and on up to the top floor, to my own room. Rob had left my bag inside, next to the bed.

I was lucky. As the only daughter I had a room of my own, while Rob and Mark still shared – and they'd never got on. After the tiny space I shared with Mistress Pyatt at Lyde Hall, my bedchamber here seemed large. The plain plaster walls had been re-decorated a few years before with a dark green paper printed with swirls of briar roses and birds. There was a chest for my clothes, and a bowl and a jug of warm water for washing. On a table near the window was my sewing basket and the book in which I made drawings and pressed flowers and kept ideas for embroidery designs. I took from the pocket of my gown the leaves and grasses I'd collected in the chase and laid them out on the linen cloth that covered the table.

I was home – in my own room, and at peace for a while.

*

It was impossible to stay unhappy – or even to think much about David – during the first two days at home. Mark, my elder brother, had good news: he was to be married at Eastertide to Grace Barber, a girl we'd known all our lives, the eldest daughter of a cloth merchant, and another secret Catholic. Mark and Grace would be moving to a house and shop of their own and setting up in business. There was also talk about my father's search for a new young apprentice to join Kit Woodings, who had been with him for several years.

On Michaelmas Day we rose early and spent an hour in private prayer before making our way, as the law demanded, to the Protestant church. I had become accustomed to hearing Mass, and now I tried to shut my ears to the sermon delivered by a minister facing the congregation and speaking in English. But one thing cheered me: there, as ever, where the whitewash didn't quite reach, was my hidden saint – St Winefride, perhaps? – stepping out on her small slippered feet, her skirt swinging forward as she moved.

We returned home for the feast. Grace and her parents and brother joined us, along with Kit (who had no family to go to), the five of us and the servants, Joyce and Bess. We were very merry and there were toasts and good wishes for Mark and Grace. Rob was still in a jaunty mood, full of suppressed excitement about something, and I couldn't help but feel my own spirits lifted. I wore my yellow gown, and Rob his fine doublet, and both were much admired. After dinner my father got out his fiddle and we sang old songs of love and adventure, of meetings and partings and faithful hearts. Kit Woodings was all smiles to see me again. I liked Kit, and I knew he liked me (when I was thirteen I had been sure I would marry him), and I thought how simple life would be if we two could settle for each other.

But the next day, when normality returned and there were fewer visitors, I felt unbearably restive at the prospect of the two more days away that Rob and I had been granted. The holiday was over. Monday was a working day, and my father and Mark and Kit were back in the shop, and I knew that at any moment David might receive the message from his contact that would set him on his journey to Gravesend and then to Paris.

Of course my mother noticed that something was not right. She cornered me in my bedchamber on Tuesday morning. "You're not happy, are you, my wench? What's wrong with you?"

"Nothing."

She persisted. "Is there someone you don't get on with? Do you want to come home? Is that it?"

"No!" My response was so sharp that I feared I had hurt her feelings. "No, I love being there: my work, hearing Mass, the other people in the house…"

She looked at me keenly. "Do you go to confession?"

"Yes." I knew I was blushing.

"It's not a man, is it?" And then she looked at my face and said, "It is, I can see. Oh, Mary, you're not…?"

"No!" I exclaimed. "I'm not. It's not that."

I couldn't tell her. To do that I'd have to betray David's secret identity.

"It's nothing," I said again. And I began to talk about the St Winefride embroidery design, and how pleased Lady Chilton was with my work – things I knew she'd be glad to hear. That set her reminiscing about her own time there, long ago, when she and the lady were both young women. She told me again what I already knew: that we two were distant relatives of the lady's family who had kept up the tradition of fine needlework. She was proud of that connection, and while she talked about it I felt safe.

But as she got up to go, she came back to her earlier theme: "There's you all of a mope, and Rob – he's fizzing with something, that's for sure. What's he up to?"

"I don't know, Mum." That was the truth.

She patted my arm. "Your father says there are neighbours and customers coming in, asking after you. You should come down and see them, show yourself in the shop."

"I will," I promised.

She left me then, and I began to wash and dress.

One more day, I thought. Today – and then tomorrow we'll go back. And David – I prayed he would still be there. I longed to speak to him. We'd parted so abruptly, and I'd been cold to him – and left him to Father Taberer.

What a fool I was! Father Taberer – that handsome, well-dressed gentleman who wore a sword and could pass for a kinsman of the lady's; a man familiar with places like Paris and Rome, who had often travelled overseas, who had exciting stories to tell of escapes from pursuivants, who was learned and could guide David in his reading and his prayers… All the time I was away he would be there, exerting his power and influence over David. I had warmed to Father Taberer immediately when I first came to Lyde Hall, but now I had come to see him as my enemy.

The day passed pleasantly enough. I helped in the

shop and talked to people who had known me from childhood; cut and rolled lengths of ribbon, advised on lace for caps – let people see that mixing with the gentry hadn't made me proud.

And at last came Wednesday, the day of our return. The talk that morning was all of the expected eclipse of the sun – Rob and my father both looking at their pocket almanacs, and everyone wondering what such a portent might mean. My mother was anxious about us travelling during an eclipse.

"We'll be back at the hall before it starts," Rob assured her. And we both said goodbye to everyone with hugs and kisses and a promise to come again soon.

We set off early, with me riding pillion behind Rob, so there was not much conversation between us. The road was less crowded than it had been on market day, and we made good time, though we passed a few travellers on horseback and in carts. Near the turn-off into the chase we encountered a group of armed men wearing the sheriff's badge. They rode past us, harness jingling, helmets glinting in the sun, and I felt the muscles in Rob's back tighten, even though they took no notice of us.

We left the road and turned onto the track through the chase. Shafts of sunlight pierced the forest cover. It was hard to believe that in an hour or two the sun would begin to lose its power, that nothing could prevent this, that the eclipse was inevitable.

Rob rode at a fast pace, whistling between his teeth. He too seemed eager to be back at Lyde Hall. But the sight of the soldiers had reminded me of Lady Chilton's questions, and when we stopped for a break and dismounted, I asked him, "Are the gentlemen planning to raise a force? Buying horses?"

He shot a look at me. "Gentlemen?"

"Your master and his friends."

I had spoken lightly, hoping it was nothing, that my fears were imaginary. But in a fierce whisper he demanded, "What have you heard? Tell me."

I began to tremble, but I wasn't about to let him see my fear.

"Some business of your master's," I said. "I overheard him talking with Stephen Littleton from Holbeach and that young gentleman – the fair-haired one."

"You should not listen to men's talk."

"I didn't! I told you, I overheard it. They were on the stairs."

"Where you had no business to be."

He was angry. Afraid. Mum's right, I thought. He knows something. Or suspects it. Perhaps he's involved in some plot to smuggle priests into England – or even to go with a force to Flanders, to fight with the King of Spain's army.

"I don't trust Francis Chilton," I said. "You've changed since you became his man. You scare me."

His face darkened, but I pressed on. "You're becoming like him, doing his bidding, aping his ways. You mix with dangerous men, outlaw priests—"

"While my sister is a priest's whore!"

It was as if he'd punched me. I began to tremble. "Don't dare call me that!"

"What else can I call you? My master told me your David's on his way to Paris. That he's with the Jesuits.

That he'll be gone soon from Lyde Hall. The lady's secretary. Isn't that what he passes as?"

"It's what he *is*." The strength had returned to my voice. "He's not a priest. Not yet."

But I felt his shock at hearing the truth about David.

"Rob, I'm afraid for you." I reached out – laid a hand on his arm.

He shook me off.

"Don't be." His voice was hard. "I can look after myself. Forget what you heard. It's no business of yours. Let's get back to Lyde Hall before the light goes."

Chapter Eleven

We could not look at the eclipse, but we knew when it had started. Although the sun still shone, its light was weaker and the day dimmed almost imperceptibly. The air grew cold. We were aware of the breathing forest around us, the brittle leaves underfoot, the piping of birds that seemed to hold a note of wariness, as if they knew.

I shivered, and leaned in closer to Rob. If only I'd never roused his anger! The eclipse felt ominous. Perhaps it had caused our quarrel. I could still feel the tension in him. We rode uphill, out of the woods, and turned onto the road that led to Lyde Hall. Here, in the open, the air struck colder. There was an eerie stillness and most of the birds had fallen silent. I risked a glance at the sun; glimpsed the shadow and the rim of fire.

Eclipse. It boded ill. Perhaps the death of a king. That was something it was treason even to imagine; such a thought must never be spoken. And King James was neither old nor sick. He had a wife and young children.

As the house came into view and we rode towards it, the thought of David rushed into my mind, and I yearned to see him and be sure that he had not left already for France. This would surely not be an auspicious time to sail, or even to travel to Gravesend. I clung to that hope, while still fearing that Father Taberer might have spirited him away in my absence.

John Frewen saw us coming and opened the gate.

"They're out back, watching the sun being swallowed up," he said. "Her ladyship and all. Me, I don't like to see it. It always brings harm. Last eclipse, my youngest took sick and died, her that was bonny as a robin till then."

His words sent a tremor of fear through me.

We dismounted, and led the horse round to the stable yard, where we found the lads taking peeks at the sun through a smoked glass.

"Leave that," Rob said curtly. "You'll burn your eyes out. See to my horse."

The gentlefolk and the upper servants were gathered in the walled garden. The gate was open, and Francis, catching sight of Rob, summoned him in. I followed, my gaze darting around the crowd in anxiety until, to my huge relief, I saw David. He turned and acknowledged me with a nod and the smallest lift of his hand. I saw that Father Taberer, who stood near him, had noticed the gesture, and my stomach tightened.

Everyone was standing in a semi-circle around something in the centre of the paved area. Henry appeared beside me. "Come and see this," he said, drawing me forward. He was kind and courteous as always, and in my shaken state I was glad to be free of Rob and go with him.

I gasped in surprise. A linen sheet had been spread on the ground, and someone had brought a colander from the kitchen and propped it up at an angle so that it caught the sun's light and cast shadows onto the sheet: an arc of dozens of tiny suns, each one a sliver with a great bite taken out of it. I gazed entranced, seeing how each hole in the colander cast a shadow. The eclipse seemed less fearful now it had become a thing of beauty.

Henry looked pleased with himself, and I realised it had been his doing.

Lady Chilton saw me and acknowledged, with a nod, my return to Lyde Hall. I bobbed a brief curtsey.

The sky was overcast, the air still; but soon we all felt a change, a turning-point. Very quickly the garden began to feel warmer. There was more birdsong. People stirred and talked together, and the lady summoned Jane and David and the three of them began making their way back towards the house. David glanced at me as he passed – a glance that warmed me as much as did the brightening air.

I followed the lady, with the other servants, at a respectful distance as we all went back to the house. In my bedchamber I washed and changed my dusty clothes, and emerged feeling fresh and smelling of rosewater. The memory of what Rob had called me could not be washed away as easily – but when I went into the sewing room Mistress Pyatt welcomed me with a kiss and asked after my family.

"You are lucky to have them," she said.

I thought of her, a childless widow, with no one to go to on holy days, and I said, impulsively, "You must come to us at Christmas. My mother would love to meet you and talk about the old days at Lyde Hall."

I had no foreboding then of what a dark place we would all be in by Christmas.

Dinner was eaten late that day because of the eclipse. In the afternoon Mistress Pyatt and I both had plenty to do, and I knew that David, too, would be at his desk, busy with accounts or correspondence for Lady Chilton, so I made use of the daylight to work on my banner. It was taking shape, and I could now begin to see how the finished design would look, and how the touches of gold thread enhanced it. I worked until the light faded and Mistress Pyatt began to wonder aloud what Master Tandy might have put aside for us.

I set off down the narrow, winding staircase, turned a corner and ran straight into David coming up. We gasped, clung together and kissed.

The kiss was long, and full of our pleasure at being reunited and not knowing when or whether we'd have another chance.

"I've missed you," he whispered. "I spent the days you were away trying to put you out of my mind, but I couldn't do it."

"*I* was afraid I'd come back and find you gone."

"I did get a message—"

"You *did...*?" Now I began to tremble.

"It came to Father Taberer. They were to have come for me next week, but there has been some problem and the rendezvous is delayed."

"So...when?"

He gave a great sigh. "I don't *know*. Father Taberer says this often happens. Everything must be right: the safe houses, the ship, the master – and then the tide... They won't risk a weak link. So they wait and try again. He says it may not be long, and" – he took a breath – "I must be ready."

All my joy at reuniting with him was gone now. "You want to go," I accused him.

He could not meet my eye. "I hate this waiting," he said. "The uncertainty – in the plans, and in myself. I feel…"

Below us, a floorboard creaked. We sprang apart and he moved swiftly past me, up the stairs. I crept down, but saw only the back view of Barbara carrying a heavy jug along the passage towards Lady Chilton's chamber. We were safe.

I had no further opportunity to talk to him. Once, when he was downstairs at work, Nell – who had been cleaning his bedchamber – went out leaving the door ajar. I peeped in, and noticed a small crucifix on the writing table that had not been there before. A rosary lay beside it. There was sheet music, too. Sacred music, I guessed, such as they sang at the seminary in Paris; the music that he loved and that could so easily lure him away from me.

I felt the hold that the Jesuits had on him, and how drawn he was to that life of prayer and study and music. Father Taberer; the Jesuit college in Paris; St Ignatius. Against such forces, what power did I have? David would be led into a life of banishment and danger, a life that would make him a traitor and a wanted man if he ever set foot in England again. Such priests were needed – priests who were brave enough to return to England in the Jesuit mission; charismatic men who could lead people into reconciliation with Christ. These priests were to be admired, loved, protected and supported. But why must David be one of them?

I vowed to myself that I would fight for him. I could – I knew I could – turn him to me if only I could find a way to be with him. I dared not go to his room.

My near-encounter there with Henry had made me feel ashamed; and Rob's harsh words had added to my distress. I thought longingly of that day in August – the day of the village wake – when David and I had run down to the stream together and walked and talked easily as young people do on the brink of love when there is all the time in the world to discover it.

But all that seemed lost now. Father Taberer had access to him, and I did not – unless I behaved in a way that would probably lead to my dismissal. The priest knew I was a threat to his plans, and I was already afraid that he might advise Lady Chilton to send me away. I needed to make sure I continued to please her, so that she would not want to part with me. But I could see no way to be with David. And at any moment he could be told the date of his own departure.

Then something happened that brought change to all our lives.

Several Jesuit priests came to Lyde Hall. They were on their way to a great house in Warwickshire where they would gather with others to celebrate St Luke's Day. They stayed with us only two nights, and because they were expert at travelling secretly they attracted no attention and we had no alarms or searches. Mass was celebrated in the sewing room and in Lady Chilton's private room. And several people went to confession. I went myself – it was a relief to me to confess to a priest who was a stranger – but in the end I could not put into words all the thoughts that troubled me, and spoke only of small sins.

On the second day, at dinner in the hall, I noticed that Rob and his master were not there.

"I saw them leave this morning," said Meg, "laden for a journey." She looked downcast.

So Rob was gone – with no word of reconciliation for me. And no kind farewell for her.

"He's not worthy of you," I said in an angry whisper.

She looked alarmed. "What has he done?"

"Nothing I know of, but…" I dared not tell her what Rob and I had talked about. "He *is* lovable," I said, "and good-hearted. He's my favourite brother. I told you – didn't I? We were the two youngest. He'd tease me, but always defend me…"

She smiled, and I saw the longing in her.

"I wish he'd…" A lump rose in my throat.

Meg put a tentative hand on my arm. "It's his master, isn't it?" she said, her voice low and cautious.

I shivered. "Yes."

The priests left next morning. One of them had become suddenly unwell – dizzy and fevered – but although Lady Chilton suggested that they stay and she call a doctor, the man was determined that they should continue on their way.

A day later Lady Chilton was taken ill. She took to her bed with shivering, dizziness and a sore throat, and by the evening she was barely able to speak or breathe and could only take small sips of wine. Jane and Elizabeth White tended to her, and a doctor was summoned from Wombourne. He bled her and recommended sage, willow bark, rest and prayer. Then Jane fell ill, and then Elizabeth and, over the next few days, Lady Vavasour and three of the household servants – Martin, Alice and the kitchen boy Ned Tolley.

Visitors were warned to stay away. In the sewing

room Mistress Pyatt took on my share of our work, and I was sent down to the still room to help Meg, who was coping alone.

I found her with Elizabeth's handwritten book of remedies open on the table beside her as she prepared a soothing concoction for the sufferers' throats.

"What's in it?" I asked.

"Honey and liquorice, mainly – and some anise."

She left me stirring it while she made up small linen bags filled with dried sage, nutmeg and bay. Later, she said, these would be heated on a hot stone by the fire till they were the right temperature to be laid on the body.

"I'm glad, now, that Rob's away," she said. "This fever is so sudden and fierce. My aunt says her throat feels like a furnace – and poor Lady Vavasour can't speak at all."

She placed three cups of the syrup on a tray for me to take upstairs for the ladies. "They must sip this slowly. You may have to dip a piece of muslin in the syrup and give it to Lady Vavasour that way."

Upstairs I found Father Taberer with the ladies. Lady Chilton and Jane were beginning to recover.

Lady Vavasour was propped up on a pillow. She was almost asleep, the breath raucous in her throat. Some of Meg's heated herbal bags had been laid on her body. Her face was blotchy. Offering her the muslin dipped in syrup was a difficult task. I held it to her lips, but there seemed to be almost no response. After a while Father Taberer came to sit with her, and it was with relief that I retreated downstairs.

That day, as on most days now, I looked around the faces in the hall at dinner and checked for absences.

David was still there. We acknowledged each other with a brief glance. I knew he would be fearful for me, as I was for him – and for Meg. But Meg and I had no fear for ourselves. We felt strong and healthy.

The following morning Father Taberer came into the still room, where the two of us were at work. He told us that he had heard Lady Vavasour's confession and given her the viaticum and that she had died shortly afterwards in peace.

Meg and I both crossed ourselves.

That evening there was a Mass for the lady's soul – the first of many.

I felt sad and shaken by Lady Vavasour's death. But we had work to do. We were needed to help the living, and Meg sent me upstairs with more herbal drinks for Elizabeth and Alice, who were on pallet beds in the sewing room under Mistress Pyatt's care.

"They are both doing well," said Mistress Pyatt. "I hope we shall see the last of this sickness now – though I hear that little Ned is still poorly."

Sunlight streamed into the room, and both women felt cooler to the touch and breathed more easily.

I was on my way back downstairs when I began to feel ill. It seemed to come from nowhere: a slight dizziness, a roughness in the throat that rapidly increased to a tight fiery pain. By the time I reached the still room on the ground floor I knew I had the fever. Meg ran to help me and took the rattling tray from my hands. I saw fear in her eyes.

I remember little of the next few days. Mistress Pyatt made up a bed for me in the sewing room and somebody – John Frewen, I think – carried me up there. I lay on a pallet, burning with fever. My throat was closed. I could only sip a little mulled wine or Meg's syrups. I slept on and off and could not speak above a whisper.

People came and went: Father Taberer, who prayed with me, and Meg, bringing poultices which she laid on my chest.

Days passed. I didn't know how many. I sipped warm ale with egg yolk in it, then progressed to oats simmered in broth. I heard voices, agitated conversation, Barbara crying.

"David…" I murmured. A great fear tormented me but I had no strength to fight it.

"He's well." Mistress Pyatt's voice. Her hand was gentle on my forehead.

"Where…?"

"Across the passage. In his room. He's not allowed in the sickroom, but he asks after you all the time."

Dimly, through the fog of fever, I remembered that Mistress Pyatt did not know of David's mission – the truth about him. But it seemed that for now he was still here, and well. Relieved, I sighed and dozed.

I was the last person in the house to fall ill. When I began to recover Mistress Pyatt told me that there had been another death: Ned Tolley, the kitchen boy, only eight years old.

"It's sad to lose such a little one," she said, "but it's often the very old and the youngest who die of these sudden fevers."

There were tears in her eyes. She had lost young children of her own. I put my arms around her and we wept together for all of them.

On the day I felt strong enough at last to get up and

go downstairs I found the household restored almost to normality. Lady Chilton thanked me for my help during the sickness, and urged me to take things slowly. At dinner in the hall I looked across the board and filled my eyes with the sight of David, and saw an answering relief in him.

Meg, sitting beside me, said, "Poor David. He's been so anxious for you – asking after you all the time."

"And Rob…?"

"Still not back." She sighed.

I reached out and took her hand.

In the afternoon Mistress Pyatt shooed me away when I tried to return with her to the sewing room. She and Barbara went up together to fumigate the room, take out the used bedding, scatter clean rushes and bring in healing herbs. I retreated to the still room, but Meg and Elizabeth would not have me working there either.

I looked out of the still room window. From there I could see the herb garden, the wall and the meadow beyond. It was late October – a golden day, the sun low, no wind stirring the leaves.

Meg said, "You could go out. Pick me some sage and rosemary?"

It was a joy to go into the garden. I remembered the summer days when Mistress Pyatt and I had sat out there with our sewing. The herb garden had died down a little now and the paths were slick with fallen leaves, but the herbs Meg needed were still growing – woody stems and sharp spikes of rosemary and soft grey-green sage leaves. I filled a small basket, then left it by the door and went into the main garden. I walked around the paths, breathing in the fresh, cool air and the earthy scents.

A few late roses were still blooming, but when I touched one – a creamy pink – its petals fell and littered the path.

I heard footsteps – and looked up to see David coming towards me from the house.

"David…" My voice shook.

"I saw you go out."

He drew me into one of the secluded places, where we could not be seen from the house. We embraced, and he kissed me gently, tenderly, as if he feared I might break.

"I thought I'd lose you," he said. "You were so very ill. And Lady Vavasour, and then the boy, Ned…the sight of Master Tandy weeping…all the prayers…"

"I was afraid I'd wake from my fever and find you gone."

He held me close. "I won't go," he said.

"Won't?"

"Mary…would you marry me?"

I stared at him. "Then you are not going to Paris?"

"No."

"Have you told Father Taberer?"

"Of course."

"What did he say?"

"Oh! He wants me to wait until the message comes – not to decide until then. *Wait!*" He gave a great sigh, and I saw how torn he had been all this time. "But I told him I had already decided. When you fell ill – when I feared you were near death – I realised how short, how fragile our lives are on this earth; that our time is now and we should seize it."

I gazed at him. I had been bracing myself to part from him – and soon. And now we spoke of marriage.

"I don't mean at once," he said. "I don't have the means and I will need to find work and establish myself. And we should seek our parents' approval. But to be promised…"

He had become aware of my silence. "Mary? What's your answer? Is it too soon to ask you? Only…I felt I had to speak, because the message could come for me any day now. And if I am to choose a secular life I would have it with you – no one else."

"And I with you," I said.

It was a promise. We kissed.

I felt sure he would stay true to me over those years before we could be married. And I would stay true to him. I loved him and would wait for him.

It seemed simple, but in my heart I knew it was not. He was giving up his vocation because he felt unworthy to be a priest. Because of me. Because I'd come between him and everything he'd been striving for.

We walked back to the house, our hands brushing.

I thought about our two families, living as Church papists – 'schismatics', as the priests call them. Could David endure that? I thought not. But he had said he would marry me; he must know that would mean compromise. And the times could change. Surely they must? This year we'd heard that the Queen had turned Catholic. And my parents, like many people, believed that the influence of the King's martyred mother, Mary Queen of Scots, was at work in him from heaven and would ensure that he returned to the true faith.

"You're quiet," David said.

"I'm thinking. This won't be easy for us, will it? Especially for you."

"We'll find a way," he said. "Don't fear. I'll take you to Shrewsbury; and my parents will love you. We'll be happy. We *will*." He bent and whispered in my ear, "We'll eat manchet every day." And we laughed.

That evening the servants assembled in the kitchen for supper. Most people usually took supper in their chambers or work places, but since the infection had broken out this had become an opportunity for all who were not sick to meet and talk. It brought us together and reinforced our trust in each other. It was also an opportunity for gossip, and there was a buzz of voices in the big stone-flagged room. People came over to speak to me, to welcome me back from the sickroom.

We sat on benches and stools around the table. A great fire blazed in the hearth, and over it hung an iron cauldron from which Master Tandy was ladling bowls of pottage and passing them along the board. There was beer, too, and bread.

He served me himself. "Here, get this down you, Mary. Get your strength back."

I was sitting with Meg on one of the benches. I saw David coming in, and we exchanged a quick glance before he went and sat with Henry. People had noticed us, of course, and one or two gave us a nod or smile. No doubt we had been seen leaving the garden together.

Mistress Pyatt came in puffing, and plumped herself down near me. "The sewing room's clean and aired now. I'll be glad to get back to things as they were. I've missed you."

The talk turned to All Souls Day, which was almost upon us.

"I doubt whether anyone will go home for it," said Master Tandy. "Not you, Mary, for sure."

I felt David's attention on me.

"No," I said. "And my brother is still away."

Kate Newey tut-tutted. "Yes, he's away with Master Francis – who you'd think would have come home now, with his mother so ill."

"Reckon he doesn't know," said John Frewen.

"Well, he'd know if he stayed home more often," retorted Kate, causing grins and shaken heads. She was always illogical, but fiercely loyal to the lady.

I knew Lady Chilton was anxious about her son and wished she knew more of what he was doing. A discussion ensued about why Francis was away so much. Visiting and hunting at other great houses was the favoured guess. The search for a wealthy bride was another. Or buying horses.

"He keeps a fine stable these days. Stallions. War horses, too. None of your ladies' mounts and nags," said Martin.

"They say Catholic gentlemen are going for soldiers, to fight for the King of Spain." That was John Frewen.

"Reckon they be raising a force to go over there?"

Kate Newey, ignoring such speculation, returned to her theme. "It's time he was married. He must be over thirty now. Time he had a wife and a home of his own."

The talk flowed on around us. David and I had declared our love for each other, but it did not yet feel like a time to share our news or to celebrate.

Later that evening, when Mistress Pyatt had begun to chivvy me to go to bed ("You're not recovered yet; don't waste your strength"), we heard men arriving below, and John Frewen opening up.

It was too dark to see, but I knew their voices: Francis Chilton and Rob.

"I must go down!" I said.

"You will not," retorted Mistress Pyatt. "Let him come to you."

But I couldn't wait. I hurried downstairs, out into the yard, and saw the two of them outside the stables. Ben and the other boy were rubbing down the horses.

"Rob!" I ran across the yard. Francis Chilton saw me, frowned, and ordered him back inside – but Rob hesitated, long enough for me to reach him. He smelt of cold and night, yet he was well-dressed as if for company at some great house.

"Little sis, you've been ill…"

"Robert!" Francis Chilton's voice was peremptory.

"I can't stay," Rob said. He looked stricken as he turned away from me.

And I'd had no chance to ask where they had been, what they had done, or when they would go again. I feared it would be soon. And I knew it was not in his power to choose.

Chapter Twelve

On Sunday the 3rd of November we rearranged the sewing room to make a church, and Father Taberer celebrated Mass. Outside, a low mist and drizzle hung over the fields and woods, blurring outlines, keeping the sky overcast and the room dark; but the tall candles filled the space with warmth and their soft light glinted on gold vessels and vestments.

I knew by now that it was the lady's practice to join the household for Mass once a month. She rarely missed it. Today she was there, but although it should have been an occasion for thanksgiving with the sickness gone from the house, she looked strained and anxious. Francis, beside her, was intent on the Mass, swift to fall to his knees, head bent in prayer, absorbed in each moment.

Rob stood behind him, and I saw that he, like his master, was deeply involved in the prayers. The two of them had the air of men preparing for some enterprise, like soldiers before a battle.

Later that day the weather worsened. Purple-grey cloud massed over Pennsnett Chase, and rain fell, steady and relentless, bringing an early dusk. Mistress Pyatt and I were at work with candles around us when we heard men's voices below and looked out to see Francis Chilton and my brother preparing to ride out. Both were armed, dressed in dark clothes, their voices quiet and tense. There was a powerful sense of purpose in the way they set off along the road and disappeared into the darkness between the trees. I could not believe they were out on any social visit. I watched until I could no longer see them but only hear the faint diminishing clop-clop of hooves. A feeling of great unease came over me and I longed to reach out to Rob, to call him back. I had not spoken to him since our brief meeting three days ago.

By this time I had recovered from the sickness and returned to my usual duties. Being so busy, I saw little of David, who was also at work, closeted with Lady Chilton and her correspondence. I had no reason to doubt him, but I didn't know what was on his mind, or what he had said to Father Taberer about our marriage. So when, on the 5th November, Father Taberer sent for me, I feared the priest would be angry. I felt sure he would blame me and think it was all my doing that David had abandoned his vocation. My breathing was fast and shallow as I knocked on the door.

We met in the room he used for confession, but this time there was no curtain to hide us from each other, and I could sense, under the priestly demeanour and the enquiries after my health, his nervousness at the prospect of confronting me. That gave me courage.

"David has heard from his courier," he began. "He has a date at last: the eighth of November. Next Friday."

"Oh!" I had long been expecting this, but now the date,

the reality of it, hit me like a punch. I opened my mouth to speak, but Father Taberer said, "No – listen. The courier will meet him here and take him to a safe house where other young men are assembling for the journey to Gravesend—"

"He won't go!" I exclaimed. "He won't! Didn't he tell you?"

"I know he had concerns that he was not worthy—"

"No! He has decided not to go." I was breathless, anxious, desperate to explain. "He made me a promise. He has promised to marry me."

He shook his head. Above the red-brown beard his lips curved in a dismissive smile.

"He did!" I cried.

"Be calm, child. You have been unwell. Sit down."

I would not sit. He was already looming over me. I would not allow him any more height.

I began again: "David will not go! He wants to stay with me. To marry me." I felt my colour rise as I added, "To live like a…like a man."

"He wants to pray and to think," Father Taberer said, his voice stern, "and I have encouraged him to do that. He must come to his own decision without your influence. You distract him from his purpose."

My breath came fast. "You treat me as if I were at fault! But David sought me out. I'm not a wanton who runs after young men. I believed he was free to court me. I didn't know the true reason why he was here, and I thought…I thought he was an honest man. I still believe he is. But *he* was in the wrong. Don't accuse me!"

I was trembling with anger, and I thought: I have forfeited my position here now; he will persuade Lady

Chilton to get rid of me and I will lose David and shame my family. But at that moment I didn't care. Every word I had said was true.

Father Taberer looked taken aback at my outburst. I was not surprised. I had been brought up to be respectful to priests. My mother would be shocked. But she'd be on my side, all the same.

"Mary," he said – and I felt his suppressed anger – "I mean no insult to your honour. But I have been teaching David and I know he is one who is destined for the priesthood. If anyone should study in Paris it is David. His gifts – his singing! That was a revelation to us when he came to Lyde Hall; we'd known nothing of his voice, which is such a joy to him and others and a gift to God. But since he met you he has become unhappy, undecided—"

"Because he loves me, and no longer wants to go!" I said.

"He doesn't know what he wants."

His certainty infuriated me. "So you tell me! But why isn't he here? Can't he speak for himself? Bring him here!"

"Be silent!" he exclaimed. A dark flush rose in his face. "I can't talk to you while you behave like this. Go back to your work. Regain control of yourself. Tell no one about the message or David's life could be in danger. Leave him in peace. And *pray*, Mary. Pray for humility and grace."

I did go back upstairs, but not to the sewing room. I was shaking. I knew that if I spoke to Mistress Pyatt I would want to tell her everything, but I could not do that without revealing the truth about David and the meaning of the message. Instead I went to my bedchamber and paced about, going over and over that furious exchange, thinking of things I should have said and wondering what would become of me now.

I don't know how long I was there, but I was disturbed by a soft tapping on the door. I jumped up guiltily and smoothed my hair and clothes.

"Come in," I said, thinking it was Mistress Pyatt.

But it was David.

"You should not be here!" I drew him in and closed the door.

He said, "Father Taberer told me you'd defied him—"

"He was so angry..." I felt tears coming and wiped them away with my hands.

"He had no right! No right to blame you!"

"He fears I will steal you away from the priesthood."

"But he should not have accused you! I told him so. We had a huge argument – shouting at each other. Half the household must have heard..."

I looked at him. "So...will you tell the courier not to come?"

He shook his head. "I can't. There is no time. And it's dangerous – every message we send to and fro risks being intercepted. I should have burnt this already..."

He pulled out the letter and showed it to me. The writing was brownish-yellow, slightly blurred.

"It was written in orange juice," he said, "and disguised as wrapping paper around some gloves. Invisible until I held it over a fire."

I saw that the letter gave the day and time – an hour after dark – for meeting, and an instruction: *"If the house is watched we will wait near the bridge over the*

Lyde brook, and from there convey you to a safe house."

"Then – what will you do?" I asked.

"I think the safest way would be to send a boy from the home farm. It must sometimes happen that contact can't be made." He chewed at his thumbnail. "Can I burn this here?"

"Yes."

I stirred the embers of the fire until they brightened, and he held the letter to the flames. We watched as it blazed and blackened and fell to ash. And all his plans with it.

"But you *won't* go?" I said.

For a heartbeat he hesitated. "No. I've thought and agonised over it; had long discussions and arguments with Father Taberer. But I've told him I won't; that I'm promised to you." He put his arms around me, held me close. "I'm sorry he blamed you."

We heard footsteps in the passage, and both tensed. If he were found in my room it would bring more trouble upon us.

We kissed. Then I opened the door, went down the steps and checked that the passage was empty.

"Go now," I said.

I should have felt happier after our meeting, but I didn't. The date was still fixed: Friday, the 8th November. The courier would still come. Today was Tuesday, the 5th. I would not feel sure of him until this week had passed.

Mistress Pyatt noticed my quietness and asked, "What did Father Taberer want?"

"Oh…I have not been to confession lately. He…he found time for me."

I wondered if anyone had heard me shouting at the priest. If they had, word would soon get around and she would hear of it. But that room was in a part of the house not much used, which was why it had been chosen for confession.

"Well, you're popular today," she said. "Barbara came by and told me Lady Warne wants to see you."

"Lady Warne?" I had feared – almost expected – a summons from Lady Chilton, but what could her aunt want of me?

"Yes. Poor old soul," said Mistress Pyatt. "She must be lonely since Lady Vavasour died. After dinner, she said. And take your embroidery with you."

Lady Warne sat close to her fire, which blazed in a great stone fireplace embellished with carvings of gryphons and heraldic lions. This was the parlour she had once shared with Lady Vavasour, and the deceased lady's pets were still there: a linnet chirping in a cage by the window, and a large tabby cat that now occupied Lady Warne's lap.

"I miss my cousin," Lady Warne said. "She was a foolish woman, but I miss her more than I expected. Bring up a stool, child. Sit down. And let me see your work."

"I have not made much progress lately," I said, as I unrolled the St Winefride banner, "because of the sickness…" I remembered Lady Vavasour and little Ned, and fell silent.

"The sickness is gone," said Lady Warne firmly. "But you are not so happy today, I think? Is it David?"

She knew, then. Did *everyone* know? Tears burned my eyes.

"Now, now," she said. "Put your work down – we don't want tear-stains – and tell me all about it."

So I did. I told her everything. Although she was a gentlewoman, and I scarcely knew her, I trusted her and felt that she understood.

Her lips twitched with suppressed laughter when I spoke of my confrontation with Father Taberer.

"It will do the Father no harm to have his feathers ruffled now and then," she said. "But you…you must not be sad. David has wronged you. He let you think that he was free to love you, when he was not."

"But now," I said, "he *wants* to be free. He has promised to marry me. He won't go to Paris."

"Are you sure about that?"

Her glance was keen and I knew she had seen through me. I recalled that heartbeat of time before David had said yes, he would stay with me. All my uncertainty and unhappiness was contained in that moment.

"I had two daughters," said Lady Warne. "And if you think the love of young men causes heartache, wait till you have children… My eldest, Dorothy, became a nun and entered a convent in France when she was nineteen. It was a great joy to me and brought honour to our family – though I missed her and have not seen her for many years. The younger one, Jocosa, whom we had hoped to see well married, ran off with our steward. Oh, it was a great scandal at the time! My husband had the pair apprehended. Jocosa was brought back in tears, but nothing would shake her in her devotion to this man. At first we refused to give her anything to take to the marriage, hoping to force them apart, but it made no difference. They loved each other, and she was with child; so we made peace with them."

"And – was she happy?" I asked, surprised but fascinated that she had related all this to me.

"She was, though she lived only a few years longer. But she lived the life she wanted. As her sister still does."

"You are telling me I should let David go," I said.

"No. But I fear that if he gives up the chance to do what he truly wants, for love of you, it could blight your love and cause bitterness between you in the future."

I thought about this. I did not want to believe it.

"Father Taberer told me I should pray for guidance," I said.

"So you should. You are named for the blessed Virgin. Tell her your troubles. She will not fail you."

"I will."

But I would not go to confession, I thought. Not to Father Taberer. How could I, now? I remembered Brother Nicholas, who had told me St Winefride's story. I'd have confessed to him, if he were here. But Brother Nicholas was not a priest, only a lay brother, and could not have heard my confession even if he had wished to.

The tabby cat yawned, stretched, sprang off Lady Warne's lap and went to sit on the windowsill.

Lady Warne smiled. "Now we can both work on our embroideries."

We stitched in silence for a while. The repetitive design of the border was soothing to my troubled mind. There was no surprise, no disturbance, only the regular pattern – leaves, starry flowers, winding stems – and the careful counting of threads.

"Today will have been a great occasion in London," remarked Lady Warne. "The state opening of Parliament. Young Francis Chilton told me it would be today. He hears all the news of Westminster. There will have been lords attending from these parts, and from all over the country. The King and Queen, and young Prince Henry, a great procession through Westminster, and a feast. It is always a grand occasion. I saw it once, years ago. Ah, well, it will be over now. And I am too old for London."

"I should like to have seen the procession," I said. "And visited London, too."

"Well, you are young. Your life is all before you. But now you must go back to the sewing room. Mistress Pyatt will be needing you."

Later that day, when the early dark was closing in, I stepped out of the sewing room with a tray of empty cups and dishes to take down to the kitchen, and saw the familiar glimmer of candlelight under David's door. It took all my willpower not to knock when I came back upstairs, but I had taken heed of Lady Warne's advice and knew I must leave him to his own thoughts. That night, in the bedchamber, I knelt and prayed, and gradually some peace came to me.

On Wednesday, the 6th of November, a tradesman calling at the kitchen told how he'd seen soldiers on the move – more than usual. "There's something afoot," he said. And he told how he'd heard that a group of armed men – and a string of horses with them – had been seen late on Tuesday night riding hard on the Dudley road.

That evening there were rumours that something had happened in London; some threat averted. A man had been arrested; others were sought. But no one knew more, or any names – at least not in the kitchen or stables.

Absorbed in my own thoughts and fears, I reasoned: if there is trouble, and so many soldiers about, then surely David's courier will not risk coming here. David and I will be free to make plans of our own…

On Thursday morning soldiers arrived at Lyde Hall wanting to check the stables. They asked about Francis Chilton – who was still away from home, along with Rob – but they did not stay long.

It was afternoon, rainy with an early dusk gathering, when Rob and his master returned. I was in the passage near the still room, where I'd been talking to Meg, and we heard them arrive and recognised their voices. I waited till Francis Chilton had gone, then waylaid my brother as he came in.

"Rob!"

He looked wild-eyed, scared, exhausted, as if he had not slept since I last saw him. His boots were mud-splashed to the thigh, his face smeared with blood or dirt – I could not see which – and he stared at me as I if were a vision from another world.

"What have you done?" I whispered. "Where have you been all this time?"

"Nothing. Nowhere." He took off his hat and ran a hand through his dark curls, dislodging dirt and twigs.

Meg had emerged from the still room and now stood beside me. I saw how shocked she was – how desperately afraid for him. She reached out a hand. "Can I fetch you anything?"

She meant a salve or some such, but he said, "Beer, if you will. I'm parched."

She hurried away.

"Come into the kitchen," I said, and laid a hand on his arm.

But he shook his head. "No. I don't want...can't talk." He yawned hugely. "Need to sleep."

Meg appeared with the tankard of beer.

He downed it almost in one breath. "Thanks. I must go. My master awaits me..." And he went out into the yard.

Meg and I looked at each other. She clutched my hand. We both trembled, and I knew that, like me, she was deeply afraid. "Something bad has happened," she said.

"Yes."

I felt a need to talk to David. It was now the 7th of November. David had told Father Taberer he would not go to Paris, but I knew his courier would come tomorrow and must be sent away.

I left Meg and hurried up the two flights of stairs.

His door was not fully closed. I tapped, softly. "David?"

No answer. I pushed the door open a little, and saw him. He was kneeling beside the chair and had neither seen nor heard me. On his face was a look of such anguish that I felt ashamed to have seen it. He appeared exhausted, pale, as if he had been praying for hours, perhaps day and night. And I knew it was because of me; because I had come between him and his chosen path. I had held him back when I should have let him fly: tomorrow, to Gravesend, to await a ship to France, as he had planned. I saw great danger, but also a whole world opening up for him that he would never be part of if he stayed safely in England with me, if he became a husband and father and endured the daily burden of trying to be a practising Catholic. Lady Warne was right. His love for me would die if it were constrained in such a life.

He looked up and saw me.

Before he could speak, I said, "You must go. Go to Paris."

At once he was on his feet, protesting.

I went in, closed the door, and faced him. "No. You *must* go. It's what you want, what you studied for. What God intended for you."

Those last words made him pause.

He looked at me, and I thought how desirable he was, how much I longed for him and how empty I would feel when he was gone.

"Yes," he said at last. "It is. It is what God intended for me."

Chapter Thirteen

That evening, as usual, I went down to the kitchen to collect a tray with bread, beer and two bowls of pottage for myself and Mistress Pyatt.

The other servants were already gathering in the hall, where they always ate supper together. I envied them this cheerful gathering and wished Mistress Pyatt was not so protective of her status and mine, and that we too could eat downstairs, as we had during the time of fever. Tonight I wanted to be part of a crowd, unnoticed, not alone with kind Mistress Pyatt commenting that I seemed downhearted and asking me questions I could not answer.

Our tray was on the table and I was about to lift it and leave when I heard a sound from outside the house: a soft boom, distant but distinct. The air vibrated, and then was still.

Everyone heard it, and looked up.

"Whatever...?"

"What was that?"

Martin ran out and opened the door to the courtyard, and most of us followed. Cool air rushed in.

I stood with Barbara and Meg, peering between the men's shoulders, looking out. There was nothing to be seen. But we all knew that what we had heard was the sound of an explosion.

"That was some way off – two, three mile, I reckon," said Martin.

We all streamed out into the dark courtyard and made for the gate that led to the meadow. I looked back and saw lights moving in the house, faces at upper windows.

From the meadow we had a distant view of forest. The sky was dark, starless, with low cloud.

"It came from the south, or south-west..." John Frewen said. "There!"

I looked where he pointed. And then we all cried out as we saw the red glow of flames rising above the tree tops.

"That's Holbeach House!" said Martin.

The other men nodded. "Could be."

"But that's no ordinary house fire – no dropped candle. That went up sudden, with a bang. Gunpowder, I'd say," said John Frewen.

By now almost everyone in the house was out and speculating on the place and cause. I saw Rob and ran to him. He was staring at the leaping flames, and I knew he was afraid.

"Is it Holbeach?" I asked him.

"Yes," he said. His look frightened me.

Francis and Lady Chilton stood apart, talking in fierce, angry whispers.

Something bad has happened, I thought, something to do with Francis and Rob and their disappearance these last few days.

I heard the steward, Master Bagnall, shout orders to send men to Holbeach House to see if help was needed, but Francis started and shook his head at that, and Lady Chilton called sharply, "No! Do nothing yet. No one must go there."

Master Bagnall looked surprised, and someone near me murmured, "'Tis unneighbourly, that. Not like the lady."

I could see that something was wrong. Francis was white-faced and stricken. Lady Chilton turned to Master Bagnall and said, "Send them indoors – all of them."

With flames brightening the night sky, we were reluctant to move, but the steward raised his voice and ordered us all to go back to our supper, and I joined the throng stumbling back across the meadow through the wet grass, the hem of my gown and my light shoes soaked through.

I felt afraid for my brother. I knew he was somehow involved in this event. What madness was he entangled in? Whatever it was, I blamed Francis Chilton and Rob's closeness to him as his servant.

As I passed the first floor on my way upstairs I heard angry voices: Lady Chilton and Francis. The lady sounded distraught, her son defensive, with an edge of fear in his voice. Father Taberer was there with them. And then the priest came upstairs and I heard him calling on David to come down.

"This is bad," Mistress Pyatt said. She laid aside her supper and walked up and down, while I stared out of the window – though it faced the road and the flames could not be seen from this side. "I don't know what Francis Chilton is caught up in, but I fear trouble for him and the lady."

And for Rob. I twisted my hands together. And David – who might also be involved, for all I knew.

"It was strange that Lady Chilton would not send men to Holbeach," said Mistress Pyatt.

For once she came with me down to the kitchen, when I took the tray back.

Everyone was talking and no one had any information. But the men were all convinced it was something to do with Francis Chilton and that news we'd heard about a man arrested in London a few days ago.

After a while Master Bagnall took charge and sent us all back to our duties and our chambers. It was late, he said; we would doubtless know more in the morning.

There was no light under David's door when we went up. He must still be with the lady and Father Taberer. Mistress Pyatt and I put away our work, tidied the sewing room and, when there was nothing more we could do as an excuse to stay up, retired to our bedchamber. We both knelt for a long time in prayer. I prayed for Lady Chilton and for David, and most fervently of all for my brother, who I feared was an innocent caught up in some wrongdoing of his master's.

I don't know what hour it was when I woke, disturbed by low, urgent voices below the window. It was still dark, and my body told me it was deep night, many hours before dawn.

I slid out of bed, careful not to disturb Mistress Pyatt, who was lightly snoring. Our window overlooked a small yard with a doorway opposite that gave entrance to the west wing. I could see the doorway, but little else because the window was so small and high. I heard one of the voices again, and recognised it as Rob's. The other must surely be Francis Chilton's. The voices fell silent, but I heard the door close, and then their footsteps, heading for the stables. So they were leaving. Where were they going at this hour? I felt full of fear for Rob. I wanted to see him – to see how he looked and find out what was happening.

The sewing room overlooked the main gate.

I darted to the door, crept out and ran barefoot in my shift down the steps and along the passage to the sewing room. I crossed to the window and looked out. But there was no sign of them. I waited, listening for the sound of the gate opening, for the jingle of harness and John Frewen's voice – but all was silent. They did not appear.

Then I understood. They must have gone out the back way, down through the meadow to the bridge over the brook and the track that led through woodland to the Dudley road.

The priests' rooms had views in that direction. I hurried out, crossed the passage and went into the end room, which I knew was unused, and pushed open the window, struggling with the stiff catch. Yes! There they were, Francis and Rob, on horseback, shadowy forms slipping quietly across the meadow where few eyes would see them. I supposed they must be armed, but they were dressed in plain dark cloaks and hats as if to pass for countrymen. I felt sure they were on the run. But what had they done? What had Rob done? I leaned out of the window, careless of the cold, watching, my hands clenched on the sill.

A sound in the room startled me. I sprang around as the connecting door to the next room swung open to reveal a white-robed figure.

I gasped in terror. A spirit? A warning of Rob's death? But even before a voice came, uncertain, "Who's there?" I had realised it was David. I ran to him with a sob.

"Mary!" His arms went round me. "You're cold. What were you doing?"

Shivering and distressed, I told him what I'd seen. He let go of me and shut the window. Then he led me through the next room and into his own chamber, sat me on the bed and wrapped a blanket around me.

"What's happening?" I asked. My teeth were chattering. "Do you know? You were with Lady Chilton this evening. She must have found out something."

He said, cautiously, "I do know a little, but I can't speak of it. It seems that a plot against the King has been discovered. They have arrested a man in London."

"I already heard something of that," I said. "They were talking in the kitchen."

"Some gentlemen from the Midlands are sought…"

I stared at him; turned cold. "Francis…?"

"He denies knowledge of a plot. But there are friends, people he knows…"

He looked uncomfortable, and I knew he was breaking confidence by telling me even this much.

"I won't repeat anything," I said. "But I need to know – what has Rob got into? My mother, father, all my family – they know nothing of this. Oh, David, what will happen to Rob?"

"Don't be afraid. It's Francis who's in danger. Rob's just a servant."

He said it to reassure me, but I knew that treason was a net that would haul in big fish and little fish alike – and innocents, too. I shook with fear.

David wrapped the blanket around both of us and held me close. I felt the heat and comfort of him through our nightclothes and clung to him, crying. He hugged and kissed me; sobbed that he must stay; he could not leave me like this, not now; I could be in danger. We should never part, never give each other up. His face was wet, salty with tears. Tears were running into my mouth and I didn't know whether they were my tears or his. He held me so hard it hurt – as if he could never let go. But it was too late. We both knew it. He no longer had a choice. And in the end it was he who drew back, saying, "You must not stay here with me, Mary."

A sound came from below: the single note of a bell.

I felt him tense. "The bell for Matins," he whispered. "Father Taberer rings it on waking."

"But it's dead of night."

"No. This is when he rises. I do, too – if I hear his bell. Most days I don't."

I forced myself to draw away from him.

"Then if this is morning," I said, "it's already tomorrow – the day you will go."

"Oh, how *can* I leave you now?" His voice broke on a sob.

"You must. I will recover, whatever happens. But you would always be restless and unhappy if you didn't take this chance."

His silence told me he knew I was right.

We stood up, and cold air flowed between us.

From the floor below came the creak of footsteps. People were stirring – and not only Father Taberer. David caught hold of me again and held me fiercely, and we had one last, desperate kiss. And then he opened the door and checked that the way was clear. I slipped out and hurried back to my own chamber, where I climbed into bed beside Mistress Pyatt and lay wide awake and sleepless for hours.

Chapter Fourteen

I woke early, dressed, and left Mistress Pyatt sleeping as I stepped out into the passage. David emerged from his room at the same time, his eyes dark-shadowed with exhaustion. We caught each other's hands and spoke in whispers.

"I've been with Father Taberer, at prayer," he said. "He gave Francis Chilton absolution last night. Of course I don't know what Francis told him, but my guess is that he had become involved in something bigger than he had first thought—"

"Treason?"

"I think so. Father Taberer will be with Lady Chilton now. He said he would tell her that Francis has fled."

"Then Francis and Rob are now hunted men?"

"Yes."

"But – but…" In my panic I struggled to breathe. "I'm sure Rob didn't know! He's not a villain. He's a loyal servant, that's all."

David hushed me. "Try not to fear. There is nothing we can do."

"I know. But…your contact?"

"Father Taberer says the man will come, but not to the house. He'll wait near the bridge—"

I started as Father Taberer himself emerged from the main staircase and saw us. I expected him to be angry at finding me with David, but he seemed relieved to see the two of us together.

He turned to me. "Mary, you know we are all in danger? That Francis Chilton has become a fugitive?"

"Yes."

"We must prepare the house – and the hides. I fear they will cross-examine people rigorously, so I will hide this time, rather than try to deceive them. David should hide too."

"David?"

"Yes. He must meet his courier, I know. But somehow he must get out."

David said, "I could go now to the meeting place – before the soldiers come."

"No. It's too dangerous. Your contact won't come till after dark, and you'd be waiting…sure to be picked up by the sheriff. And they'll search the home farm too." He frowned. "We'll put you in the hide in the brewhouse passage. It's not the most secure hide, but it has two entrances – one from the door in the cupboard and one from the room above."

David nodded, and Father Taberer looked at me with more kindness than I had seen from him of late. "David will be safer on his way to Gravesend than he is here," he said.

From below we heard voices and movement.

"The news will soon be spreading through the house,"

said Father Taberer. "We must prepare for an assault. Master Bagnall and John Frewen will make sure that none of the conspirators is allowed in. Lady Chilton was clear about that. No one, she said."

Not even her own son. That was what she meant. And not my brother either.

He left us then, and David and I separated and went to our work. I told Mistress Pyatt all that had happened – and was about to happen.

"Oh, the poor lady!" she exclaimed. "To know that her son is the cause of this! Now, Mary, don't fear, Rob will not suffer if they're caught. It's Francis they want."

But if Francis and Rob resist, I thought – if Rob stands by his master – he could be shot and killed. I had to force myself not to imagine the worst as Master Bagnall arrived to tell us that the gates were shut and we must expect trouble. "The posse comitatus will be on the road, hunting down fugitives," he said. "They are sure to come here. Father Taberer will go into the staircase hide, with food and drink in case of a long siege. All signs of Catholic worship must be hidden away."

We had not long to prepare. It was late morning when a horseman from Holbeach – Stephen Littleton's young groom, whom I recognised from our musical gathering in September – came galloping up through the meadow to the side gate of Lyde Hall. We heard the sudden clamour of voices below, and I ran downstairs, followed more slowly by Mistress Pyatt. We joined the servants at the courtyard door as the wild-eyed lad sprang from his horse and hollered to be let in.

"I have orders to allow no entry." John Frewen's voice came from the passage behind me.

"It's only Gib, the stable lad," said Martin.

"I bring news from Holbeach!" shouted the boy. And at that Master Bagnall, who had come hurrying downstairs, ordered John to unlock the side gate and let him in.

We all gathered around him in the kitchen, and Nell brought him a mug of beer. He stood there spattered with mud, gulping the beer, and trembling, his voice full of alarm and fear and a hint of self-importance at being the centre of attention.

"There's a great force of soldiers – hundreds of 'em – come to Holbeach, armed with muskets," he said. "My master's gone – went last night – fled, or gone for help, I don't know which, or why. Yesterday, around dusk, he rode in with a group of gentlemen, all affrighted and alarmed. Pouring rain and cold, it was, and they lit a great fire, and Thomas – the serving man – he told me afterwards that they'd had gunpowder with them that had got damp from the rain, and they laid it near the hearth to dry—"

"Gunpowder?" exclaimed Master Bagnall. "By the *fire?*"

The boy nodded. "Yes, sir. By that time my master – him and another gentleman – had already gone. Reckon a spark caught the gunpowder. I was in the stable loft when the explosion came. Blew the roof of the house off."

"That'll be what we saw last night," said Master Tandy. "Said it was an explosion, didn't I?"

"Were they killed?" asked Nell.

"Not all of 'em. We heard screaming and yelling. Some of the gentlemen were hurt bad. None of us knew who they were, or why they were there, but we had" – he drew breath – "we had a great fear that they were planning some wickedness – though my master's a good man, I tell you, always been good to me. I wish he had come back. I was so scared! I didn't know any of those people. I could tell from their talk that they expected trouble. And it came – this morning. There's a battle going on there now, the wounded gentlemen holed up inside, the soldiers outside, shots exploding, smoke, fire – I reckon they'll all be killed. They're making a last stand."

Questions burst from the Lyde Hall men: "Did you hear any news of Francis Chilton?" "How big is the sheriff's force?" "Are they searching for weapons?"

He shook his head and took another swallow of beer. "I don't know. I just fled. They are desperate men, and hurt so bad, and my master gone. I saddled up one of his horses and came straight here to bring the news. I was scared to go along the highway, so I escaped out the back and came up through the chase and the meadow."

He began to cry then, smearing smoke-blackened hands across his face. "Can I stay here, Master Frewen? I'm feared to go back there with my master gone and the battle raging."

"You can't, Gib, I'm sorry," said John Frewen.

"You wouldn't be safe here, lad," said the steward. "This house has connections with Holbeach. The sheriff knows that. You would be arrested and questioned—"

Gib looked around wildly. "But I don't know anything!"

"All the more reason not to be caught here."

"You got anywhere else to go, Gib?" Martin asked encouragingly as the boy gulped and wiped his eyes.

"My mother lives in Wombourne."

"Then go there," said Martin. "Lie low till this blows over."

Gib nodded. "Should I take the horse?"

Martin looked at Master Bagnall, who nodded. "Yes. I'd say take it and ride fast."

"I'll go home, then. My mum'll hide me."

"God go with you," said Martin.

I thought of the armed might of the county out there on the roads, and pitied him. And I thought of Rob, another fugitive. And David, who planned to escape tonight. I was desperate to see David, to talk to him, to hold him in my arms one last time.

When the steward had gone, and Gib was on his way, Master Tandy looked around at us all and said in a low voice, "This matter must be treason, no doubt of it now. Nothing else would make the lady order us to lock out her own son."

Alice wiped away tears. "I wish we could have kept Gib here," she said.

"We'll have enough trouble of our own to worry about soon," said Martin.

Chapter Fifteen

We heard them before we saw them: hoof-beats, harsh voices, the jingle and clink of horse trappings and weapons. That gave us the time we needed to get Father Taberer and David into their hides with food and beer to sustain them if necessary; and to hide any incriminating books, crosses and rosaries. No evidence means no proof, so we played safe and hid everything. We knew they were hunting Francis Chilton and would tear the place apart to find him. And when they did not find him here they would fan out across the countryside, knocking on the door of every known recusant. The terror would last until they had rounded up all the suspects.

I helped Mistress Pyatt put away all signs of Mass in the sewing room – candles, prayer books, chalice, altar stone – and drag a table over the hiding place in the floorboards.

"But what *happened* in London?" I asked.

She spread her hands wide. "I don't know."

Even now, no one knew, except that another Catholic plot must have been uncovered and that desperate men were on the run. Several such plots had been foiled in recent years, but none had come so close to home.

I'd had no time to be alone with David, but Father Taberer had involved me in the preparations to hide him and I knew he trusted me to help him get away. David had packed his few possessions into a soft leather bag – rain-proof and light to carry – and tucked it out of sight behind the herb garden wall. It contained books and rosary as well as a change of clothes. The lady and Father Taberer insisted that he hide indoors – the barns and outhouses being too easily searched or even fired. When it was dark he would creep out into the herb garden and go down the meadow to the bridge, where his contact should be waiting with horses.

That was the plan. We feared it might not be so easy.

My part was also to go into a hide.

Father Taberer had chosen two connected hides for David and me. My first floor hide was a shallow box-shaped space in which a man could not even stand upright, entered via a trap door in the floor of the room that we used for confession. Directly below it was the ground floor hide – a space at the back of a broom cupboard in the narrow passage between the kitchen and the brew-house. This cupboard must once have been a pantry, for at the other end was a small window onto the herb garden, just big enough for a man to squeeze through. The two hides were connected by a second trap door in the floor of one and the ceiling of the other. Father Taberer had tested the trap doors and the ease of moving up or down between the two hides. The ground floor hide would be dangerously easy to discover if a searcher knocked on what seemed to be the back wall and found it hollow. But the room was well cluttered with mops, brooms and buckets. It must serve.

David went straight into the ground floor hide. He would only climb up into the space above if searchers began to investigate the cupboard. When we heard the banging on the door and the shouts of "Open up, in the King's name!" he was already in place.

I was upstairs with Mistress Pyatt, and heard John Frewen trying to delay their entry. Soldiers rode up and formed a great throng outside: maybe forty or fifty men. As John was forced to open up, most of them surged in under the archway, into the courtyard, but we saw how others broke away to move around both sides of the house, surrounding the barns, granary and stables. Their speed and determination terrified me. I thanked God we had not hidden David anywhere out there.

Two floors below us they burst inside, shouting for Francis Chilton to be handed over to them.

Mistress Pyatt fell to her knees and began praying. I had never seen her look so afraid, and a violent trembling almost overwhelmed me as I readied myself for my next move.

This was not like the raid we had experienced when I was new to Lyde Hall. This time the sheriff's men had a purpose, an enemy; they believed Francis Chilton to be guilty of treason and his mother to be hiding him.

I knew I must not be caught. Without a word to Mistress Pyatt, who did not know of my mission, I darted out of the sewing room, down the back staircase to the first floor, and along the passage to the spare room that lay above David's hiding place.

From the floor below I heard the lady's protests as she went to confront and delay the searchers: "There is no need to tear my house apart! He is not here. I don't know where he is." Then a man's voice that I recognised as Thomas Jevons', giving orders: "Round them all up. Servants below; ladies in the upper chamber. Guard them. Guard all doors. No one is to leave. Cover the whole house – every room, every wall, every ceiling. Find him!"

There was no time to be afraid. I lifted the heavy trap door, climbed into the small dusty space, and manoeuvred the door back in place over my head. Footsteps sounded in the passage outside.

I crouched, trembling, in the dusty darkness, afraid to move, afraid even to breathe, listening.

Boots, up and down the passage. Then a great bang on the door – I heard it fly open and hit the wall. The boots tramped around the bed, and I knew that the man would be pulling back its curtains, hauling up covers and mattress, kneeling and peering underneath.

"No one here." It was a grunt to himself. He pushed something – a stool, probably, and it scraped horribly over my head. Then he was still. Thinking? Noticing the trap door? I knew the trap door was not easy to see, but had I pulled it back so that it fitted exactly? I had to fight a longing to reach up and check.

Then came a sound I recognised: he was pissing. Probably into the fireplace – the pig.

He sighed pleasurably and, a moment later, went out.

At last. I let out a slow breath and tried to ease myself into a more comfortable position. There was a piece of sacking on the floor, which I folded and sat on. In one corner was a small chamber pot. I hoped fervently that I would not need to use it. An old, musty smell of stale body odours and excrement pervaded the enclosed space. Cramped and fearful, I thanked God for the thin square of daylight I could see around the edges of the trap door.

In the distance I heard thuds, crashes, splintering wood, swearing and occasional whoops of glee. Then sudden noise erupted outside my room, and I heard men going along the passage, knocking on walls, breaking through lath and plaster. There was a prolonged crash that sounded like a ceiling coming down. My door was flung open again and two men came in. A voice said, "Someone's done this one," but they tramped around anyway, opening a chest of linen, by the sound of it, and tossing stuff out. One of them stood on my trap door and I saw it move slightly and held myself still, scarcely breathing.

Beneath me, with only another trap door to separate us, David must be able to hear all this. I longed to be down there with him.

I thought of Father Taberer, alone in the staircase hide. If he was found he would be charged with treason and suffer a hideous death.

And Rob. Where was *he*? Was he safe? I knew he could be lying dead somewhere. I pushed that image away. I would not think of it.

The passage outside grew quieter, though I could still hear faintly the destruction that was taking place in the house. Perhaps they had moved along to the west wing where Francis had his own rooms? I put my hand on the floor and thought of David, so near. And I felt under the sacking and traced the outline of the trapdoor that lay between us.

I felt something else there: a rosary, made of smooth wooden beads on a leather thong. I began to pray the rosary, silently, only my lips moving, as the beads slipped through my fingers.

After a while I became aware that the light was fading from around the edges of the trap door above me. I felt stiff and cramped. The soldiers were still in the house. I heard voices, more banging and shouted orders – but there was no sound from David, directly below me.

Soon the light was gone. If it was dark outside in the meadow David's contact should be waiting near the bridge.

I knocked cautiously but firmly on the floor of my hiding place.

No sound.

"David?" I said, softly but distinctly.

"Mary?" It was a gasp of relief. I must have alarmed him with my knocking.

"Is it safe to come down?" I whispered.

"Yes."

I crouched at the edge of my hide, eased up the trapdoor and placed it to one side. Darkness gaped below me. Then a hand reached up, and I touched it.

"The ladder is here," he whispered. "Feel it?"

"Yes."

I pulled the trapdoor back into place above my head, then climbed down backwards, his hands guiding me.

"Last step now."

I was down. I turned around, but could not see him. The space was dark. I sensed that he was beside me, standing, in a narrow, confined space. Gradually I began to see. There was just enough room for us to stand facing each other without touching the walls on either side. He took my hand, and kissed it, and I ached with the pain of losing him.

But it was time to go.

A faint rectangle of light showed me the outline of the low door. I knew it was a flap, hinged at the top, and that we would have to crawl out.

"I'll check the way," I said.

The door lifted smoothly, and I crawled through and paused, my heart pounding. No one was there. I saw only the ghostly shapes of brooms and pails. At the far end of the room, I knew, was the shuttered window. I picked my way carefully towards it, terrified of making a sound. Behind me, David crouched at the entrance to the hide.

Father Taberer had told me he'd freed the shutters, but they still seemed stiff and creaked alarmingly as I pushed them open. Cold, damp air flowed in. Outside was the dark of field and woods; no stars. I could hear rain pattering on leaves and see the line of the herb garden wall.

I caught up my skirts, clambered onto the sill, and lowered myself into mud and prickly leaves; waited, heart pounding.

From around the corner, in the courtyard, I could hear two soldiers talking together and cursing the rain. They hadn't heard me. No one else was in sight.

"Now," I signalled to David.

He moved with extreme caution across the cluttered room; then, in a swift, decisive movement, he was up, over the sill, and out, had seized his bag from its hiding place and made straight for the wall. He glanced around, threw the bag over, and sprang after it.

I followed more slowly, hampered by my skirts, and dropped down beside him. We crouched by the wall, pressed back against it, looking and listening, all our senses alert.

Rain, wind soughing in the tree tops, the death shriek of some small prey animal. It was a foul night, and that could help us. We both stared down the meadow towards the bridge. I could see nothing – but I knew that the man, if he was there, would not show a light or reveal himself. He was probably near the bridge, under the willows, waiting, with horses.

David turned to me. He stroked my face, brushed away rain and tears, and kissed me.

"Thank you, my love," he said.

"I'll come with you to the bridge."

I wanted to stay with him till the last possible moment. I can't bear this, I thought. I can't bear it if we part here.

But he whispered, "No. I'll be safer alone. Quicker. Go back inside."

We put our arms around each other for the last time, clung and kissed. His face was wet against mine; our tears mingled. Then he seized his bag and, crouching low, ran down the meadow, much faster than I could have done in my tangling skirts. Despite the dark, moonless night I saw him almost until he reached the bridge, and then he disappeared from view.

I waited; strained to hear. I thought perhaps I heard a horse – a faint whinny – but could not be sure. And try as I would I could not see the bridge, only the dark mass of woodland beyond it. Had he gone?

This was unendurable. I had to know; had to be sure he was safely away, that the man he had met was not false, not a pursuivant in disguise; that he had not been seized and abducted. Bent low, I crept along the line of the wall, moving cautiously down the meadow towards the stream. Then, like a scared rabbit, I bolted across the open stretch of grass until I reached the willows. From there I could see the bridge.

And of course it was empty, the path beyond it dark. No sign of a struggle. No sound except the rain. Nothing.

Except...where I crouched, under the trailing leaves, there was a smell of horses. So someone had been here, waiting.

I realised I'd been hoping to find a trace, a sign left behind, perhaps even some token for me. He was gone – safely away – and for that I was glad. But now all the joy and excitement of our love was over. The thought of never seeing him again was unbearable.

I stayed hidden under the willows, empty, numb with loss. All around me was the hiss and patter of rain – fine, relentless rain that drenched my hair, my gown, my shoes. I shook with cold, but could not bring myself to move.

When at last I forced myself to stand up, my legs were stiff and my hair had come unpinned and hung in wet strips around my face. I began moving back towards the house, hunched over so as not to be seen, terrified of alerting the soldiers and setting them on David's trail. I reached the wall near the house, climbed over it and dropped down into the herb garden with a huge sense of relief.

But when I ran to the window and fumbled with the catch I found that someone had closed the shutters from the inside.

In panic I ran around the corner into the courtyard; and at once a lantern swung, startlingly bright, above me, and a hand seized my shoulder.

"It's a woman!"

Rain glinted in the circle of light. I saw soldiers, a horse – a horse with a dead body slung over the saddle –

"No!" I shrieked.

The man hung head down, arms dangling, and I saw, as weakness swept through me, that it was not David, as I'd instantly thought; and not Rob. This man wore a brown jerkin and had lank flaxen hair, splashed with mud.

I knew him then. He was Gib, the young groom from Holbeach – the boy we'd refused to shelter and had sent on his way to Wombourne only hours ago.

"Is he dead? Why did you kill him?" I cried, as they hustled me towards the back door of the house; but no one answered.

Instead I heard a familiar voice: "Mary Wilshaw?"

Thomas Jevons stepped out. "I hardly recognised you," he said.

He looked me over. I knew how I must appear. Wet, shivering, teeth chattering with shock and cold, my gown clinging to my body and my hair hanging down my back, I was at his mercy. But I would not quail before such a man. I glared at him and demanded, "Why have you murdered this boy and brought him here? What harm can he have done you?"

He was not so easily thrown off course. "Where have you been, Mistress Wilshaw?"

"I can't tell you."

"Can't? Or won't? You know we are searching for Francis Chilton? And for his servant, Robert Wilshaw – your brother."

He glanced towards the darkness of woods and meadows. "Is your brother out there, Mary? Are you shielding him? Do you know where Francis Chilton is?"

"No!" I exclaimed. "No, I don't know anything. I wish I did. I am afraid for my brother."

"So you should be," he said. He took hold of my elbow and pushed me ahead of him as he strode towards the wall.

"Light!" he shouted, and the soldier with the lantern swung it out, illuminating an area of empty meadow and falling rain. Dogs began barking in the yard behind us.

"Move it around! Over there – and there!"

The lantern beam cut the darkness. When the light swung in the direction of the willows and the bridge, I thought I would faint with fear for David. Jevons knew this place. He'd been here at the wake, seen the lie of the land. He would think of that bridge; he would surely think of it, and send men on what he guessed was Francis Chilton's trail. I could only hope that David's guide, with his local knowledge, would be able to shake off any pursuit, and that their safe house was near.

"Get men out there," Jevons ordered. "Look around."

I saw what it would mean for him – praise, and probably promotion – if he could capture Francis Chilton. As orders were shouted and men sent out, Jevons turned back to me and regarded me suspiciously. "Were you looking for him out there? Or hiding him?

Were you contacting someone? Who did you meet, Mary?" His voice rose. "Who?"

I changed tactics, and allowed tears to slide from beneath my eyelids. They came easily enough. "I was afraid when you all burst in," I said. "I ran into the herb garden to hide…"

Of course he didn't believe me. But he was becoming weary of me, and the men in the meadow were already calling out that they could see no one there. "Go upstairs," he said. "Boyce!" A soldier nearby sprang to attention. "Take Mistress Wilshaw upstairs and put her with the women in the great chamber."

"There is a fire there," he told me. "Dry yourself. We will talk again, later."

The soldier led me up the back stairs. On the way we stumbled through a rubble of broken wood, plaster and dust. A huge hole had been smashed in one side of the staircase – no doubt part of the search for hides.

"In here," the man said, opening a door to the great chamber.

A group of women, both gentry and servants, had been herded inside. The ladies and their maidservants were in a huddle together near the fireplace, while Meg, Elizabeth and Mistress Pyatt stood by the windows, looking out.

Mistress Pyatt turned and uttered a cry of shock at the sight of me, which drew the attention of everyone in the room. "Mary," she said, in a lower voice, as I joined her, "what's happened to you? Where did you go? One minute you were there, and the next…" Her eyes welled with tears.

I began to apologise, though not to explain, but she drew me towards the fireplace.

"Get dry and warm, girl! Your lips are blue."

Lady Chilton caught my eye as I stood by the fire, absorbing its welcome heat. Her face was pale and she seemed to have aged overnight. She looked a question at me and I gave the briefest of nods, which she acknowledged silently. "Meg!" she called. "Give Mary some wine – and help her to dry herself. Take off that wet gown, Mary."

Meg helped me to remove the gown and drape it over a fire screen, where it soon began to stink of wet wool. I stood there in my shift and a shawl that Jane offered me – barefoot, since my stockings and shoes were soaked. In the midst of my distress I thought what strange times these were, when a servant could appear like this in the presence of gentlewomen.

The wine was in a jug by the fire, along with bread and meat. The sight of the food made me realise how hungry I was.

I sipped the hot, spiced wine and felt warmth flowing back into me.

"Where have you been?" Meg whispered. "We've all been asking about you."

I shook my head – and she accepted that.

"They've rounded everyone up and locked them in two or three rooms," she said in a low voice, glancing at Lady Chilton. "They've made havoc here, searching for Francis, knocking great holes in the walls and ceilings, pulling up floorboards, opening chests and throwing stuff around…"

"Have they found Father Taberer?"

"I don't think so."

"They killed the boy from Holbeach," I said.

"I know."

"But – why?"

"Maybe he just looked suspicious, fleeing on that fine horse."

It was late when at last we were released and the soldiers left. We peered out through the leaded windows of the great chamber as they assembled and rode off into the darkness. All around the room people murmured prayers.

"They will be back," Lady Chilton warned. "I think Master Jevons" – she spoke his name with contempt – "would have been in here, crowing, if they had found Father Taberer. So we must hope our priest is safe. But they will be back to question us."

Our first task now was to release Father Taberer. Mistress Pyatt and I hurried upstairs.

The staircase hide was still closed, though the wall of the cupboard nearby had been smashed in. We hurried to open up, calling to the priest, and he climbed out. I remembered the last time we'd done this. He'd been confident and smiling then. Now, I saw fear in his eyes.

He turned to me and spoke quietly. "Is David…?"

"On his way."

"God bless you, Mary."

We held each other's gaze for a moment, and I thought: he is a difficult man to be obedient to, but we can't afford to be enemies.

Mistress Pyatt watched this exchange but asked no questions. "You'll want supper, Father," she said. "They'll be preparing something for you."

"Yes. I'll go down. But first I must speak to the ladies."

Mistress Pyatt and I hurried to our workroom – where she gave a cry of distress. "Look what they've done!"

Tables and stools had been dragged out of place; silks, linen, sewing things, spools of thread tossed about –

"They've found the hiding place!" I said.

The strewing herbs that covered the floor had been swept aside, and the loose boards usually hidden by my chair had a dust-free line around them. I knelt and opened up the space.

Everything was gone: the chalice, the pyx, the altar stone, the candlesticks. They had proof, now, that this room had been used for Catholic Mass.

From my position down there, kneeling on the floor, I saw the little grey cat cowering behind a fold of the curtain. I went to her and stroked her, but she would not come out.

I stood up and looked out at the darkness and the wind-tossed trees. Something glinted and moved below: a guard on the front gate shifting position.

Rob. David. Both were out there; both fugitives. Would they end up like poor Gib?

I began to shake.

Mistress Pyatt put an arm around me. "Come and get something to eat. You'll feel better."

Meekly, I followed her downstairs.

On the first landing she paused and said, "David is on his way to become a priest, isn't he? Gone to France?"

"Yes." There was no point now in keeping it secret.

"A few young men have passed through here on that route," she said. "I did wonder about David. But it's better not to know some things. Let's go down, or there won't be anything left."

In the kitchen there was warmth, food and drink. But people were nervous, whispering.

"There are guards on all the gates."

"No one can get in or out. We're prisoners."

I told them about the disappearance of the things we kept hidden for Mass.

"Is Father Taberer safe?" Master Bagnall asked me.

"Yes. He's in the great chamber."

"Keep him upstairs. The guards may notice if there's a new face down here. He must go into the hide again as soon as the sheriff's man comes back."

"But what has happened out there?" Martin exclaimed. He struck the table with his fist. "We need news!"

He was immediately hushed by the others. With guards on every door and a long winter night enfolding the house and grounds, there was no hope of any news reaching us yet, but we all felt sure that Thomas Jevons and his men would be back.

Chapter Sixteen

"I have a warrant for the arrest of your brother, Robert Wilshaw. Where is he?"

"I don't know, sir."

I was alone with Thomas Jevons, apart from a guard by the door. The room Jevons had chosen for this interrogation was one of Francis Chilton's – a room I had never visited before and where I felt anxious.

"You met him yesterday, near the Lyde brook."

"No, sir. I did not."

"Then who *did* you meet?"

"No one."

"Don't lie to me." Jevons' face was hard. "What were you doing out there?"

"I told you. I was terrified when all the soldiers came and I ran out to hide."

"In the rain?"

"Yes. I was too frightened to think."

"I don't believe you are ever too frightened to think, Mary Wilshaw. And if you don't give me answers I will have you arrested and questioned in Stafford jail. We will find those two. I have sent men to search your father's house—"

"No!" I thought of my parents, all unknowing, the terror this would bring to them. "Oh, please, sir, spare my parents!"

"Give me answers, and I will."

"I *have* no answers! My brother is Francis Chilton's servant. He does his master's bidding." I switched from entreaty to attack. "What is this crime that Francis Chilton is accused of? What happened at Holbeach? What has happened in London?"

His look was stony. "I am the interrogator here, Mistress Wilshaw. Tell me what goes on in your sewing room when it is not in use. Your priest celebrates Mass in there, does he not? Have you heard Mass in that room?"

"No, sir."

"You are lying. Where is your priest?"

"We have no priest."

"Then who celebrates Mass?"

"No one. We have no priest."

"You lie. Where is he hidden? Your priest?"

"He is not hidden."

"Ah! So there is a priest?"

"No!"

He would trap me in my lies before long. My breath came fast and shallow. Who else were they interrogating? Would someone give way? Everyone in the household had been rounded up, then separated, and threatened with interrogation.

He fired more questions at me: had I overheard anything suspicious, he asked? I thought of the whispered exchange I'd heard on the stairs between Francis Chilton and some of the visitors. I blocked the words and the memory of their faces from my mind, fearing he would see that I knew something. But who *were* these men I was protecting? What were they accused of?

"Who came to the evening of music that Lady Chilton held in September?" he asked.

It was as if he had read my mind and I had led him straight to that evening.

"Gentlefolks, sir. I don't know their names."

I was glad, now, that I had not been told.

"Can you describe any of them? Can you remember?"

Everything from that night was luminous in my memory. I recalled the visitors: our neighbour, dark Stephen Littleton; the young fair-haired gentleman; the older man – the Jesuit leader – and the lady Mistress Pyatt had said was his protector; Brother Nicholas, the carpenter; and others. Most of all I remembered the music, and David singing, and my love and longing for him.

I shook my head. "I was kept busy. I didn't see much."

"Try to bring them to mind, Mistress Wilshaw," he said, with a warning note of menace in his voice.

"I cannot remember them, sir."

When at last he released me, I fled to the bedchamber I shared with Mistress Pyatt, only to find that it had been searched, and all our possessions thrown about.

Mistress Pyatt was there, restoring order. I tried to emulate her calm as I folded and put away my gowns and shifts. But my rosary had been taken, and my Book of Hours that I'd had since I was a child. Evidence, I supposed. My hands began to shake. Rob, and now my parents...how could I protect them all from the storm that was coming?

"They can't have found Francis yet," Mistress Pyatt said. "Let's go down to the kitchen. There may be news."

But down below we found still more confusion and fear.

Alice was crying, her face blotched red. She had been bullied into admitting that Masses had been celebrated in the house; that a Jesuit priest had been present. She had confessed to hearing Mass herself.

"It's not her fault. She's only fourteen – couldn't stand up to them," Barbara told us. "At least she didn't know where we'd hidden Father Taberer. That's a blessing."

But they'll put two and two together, I thought, and they'll remember the gentleman – Lady Chilton's convenient 'cousin' – who has not been seen here lately. And I knew then that nothing would ever be the same again at Lyde Hall. Lady Chilton would lose not only her son but also her priest. She could no longer protect Father Taberer, who would need to move on – and quickly. And with those losses she would be cut adrift from much of the life that had sustained her.

We were all of us, even the ladies, held against our will at Lyde Hall, the Sheriff having ordered that no one was to leave or enter until Francis Chilton was found. But over the next two days rumours spread among the local inns and farmhouses, and secret letters must have been passing between the great households in the area. There was talk of arrests taking place all around the Midlands, and in London. At last, on Tuesday the 12th November, Master Bagnall called everyone together in the hall to hear the latest news.

When Mistress Pyatt and I arrived, the long room was already packed with people. The table and chairs had been pushed back and, in addition to the indoor staff, Master Bagnall had called in the grooms, the gardeners, the handymen, and a young man from the home farm.

Mistress Pyatt and I squeezed our way through to the middle and joined Elizabeth and Meg and the musicians. Meg and I hugged each other, mutely sharing our fear. There was no sign of either of the two ladies, nor of Jane Shenton. Soldiers stood guard at both doorways.

The buzz of talk ceased when Master Bagnall raised his voice and called for silence.

"Lady Chilton has asked me to call you here to put an end to rumour and to tell you the truth as far as we know it. You will know by now that last week, in London, a plot against his Majesty the King was foiled, and that a man has been questioned in the Tower. This man is Guido Fawkes, a Yorkshireman and a Catholic, latterly serving as a soldier in the army of the King of Spain in the Low Countries. Guido Fawkes was arrested at midnight on the 4th November in a cellar directly under the House of Lords. He was found there with thirty-six barrels of gunpowder and a fuse..."

A gasp went around the room, followed by a roar of voices. The steward held up his hand for silence and continued, "Enough gunpowder to blow up not only the House of Lords but most of Westminster. His intention was to wait there until the King and Lords assembled the next day for the State Opening of Parliament and then to light the fuse and make his escape—"

The hall erupted with sound.

"The Queen, too?"

"The Queen and Prince Henry. And all their servants—"

"Folk like us!" That roused them.

"Silence!" roared John Frewen – and Master Bagnall continued, "What has been uncovered is a plot to assassinate the King and Queen and the crown prince, and then to raise a rebellion in the Midlands—"

At that mention of the Midlands, a murmur ran through the company, and I tensed in fear. This was where the far-off London plot came home to us, where my brother was drawn in.

"Robert Catesby was the leader." Master Bagnall had to raise his voice.

"Quiet!" said John Frewen again.

"Catesby and the other conspirators had agreed a rendezvous at Dunchurch – that's east of here, beyond Warwick. From there they were to launch their rebellion. Stephen Littleton was one of the conspirators who rode to Dunchurch that night; another was Francis Chilton."

Now a hubbub burst forth, and it was all John Frewen could do to silence them.

Master Bagnall continued, "When the conspirators from London arrived at Dunchurch they brought news that all was discovered. It was then that many of those gathered there slipped away and went home. But a small group remained, determined to fight on."

"Oh, Rob..." I murmured. He'd stayed behind, in the thick of it.

"They rode to Warwick Castle, raided the stables and stole horses. For several days they must have moved from place to place, seeking a hideout in one of the great Catholic houses—"

A clamour of voices broke out. I shook my head angrily, willing them to silence. Rob? Where was Rob?

"It seems all doors were shut against them," said Master Bagnall, "and at last a small group rode with Stephen Littleton to his home at Holbeach. Francis Chilton must have lost heart by then, for he came home to Lyde Hall. Later that night, as you know, Holbeach House was blown up; and, later still, Francis rode out and has not been seen since. The next day the Sheriff of Worcester laid siege to Holbeach, and we at Lyde Hall were raided later that day."

He raised his voice again as the hall filled with sound. Everyone was talking, calling out questions.

"You will all understand that Lady Chilton is in great distress. She knew nothing of her son's activities. Francis Chilton is now being hunted. The Sheriff suspects the lady of harbouring him or of knowing where he is. This is why we are all detained—"

"But when can we go home?" demanded Kate Newey. "I've told them I'm just a day worker but they won't let me go. 'Tis all very well for the Sheriff – and I'm sorry for the lady – but I've got a family at home, a cow and chickens to feed...a place doesn't run itself, you know—"

"We can't tell you, Mistress Newey," Master Bagnall began as several people hushed Kate.

I clenched my fists. I'd have hit her if she'd been near me. Master Bagnall, too, with his 'Francis came home' and 'Francis rode out'. In a voice I didn't recognise as mine I shouted, "Well, I've got a brother out there somewhere, who's no rebel, no traitor, and I don't know where he is or even whether he's alive or dead – and everyone talks about how Francis Chilton has done this, and done that, but no one has even *mentioned* my brother yet!"

This, to my surprise, raised a clamour of support. But Master Bagnall could not give me any comfort. "Your brother will be with Francis Chilton," he said. "It's not Robert the Sheriff is seeking, but—"

"But he could be shot, or beaten, or already dead in a ditch somewhere," I said.

"I fear he could. We can't help him unless he comes back here."

The meeting broke up soon after. Mistress Pyatt and I should have returned to the sewing room, but nobody felt like work, and we were swept along with the general movement towards the kitchen. Master Bagnall made his escape, no doubt to report back to Lady Chilton, but the rest of us crowded into the stone-flagged room.

"Well!" said Master Tandy, pouring beer and passing jugs around, "that come as a surprise, didn't it, about the gunpowder!"

"Imagine it," said the head gardener, whom I'd always thought a peaceable sort, "all those Protestant lords blown sky-high! That would have been a sight!" And he laughed, and the young grooms joined in.

"Aye," said Master Tandy, "there would have been satisfaction in it."

John Frewen agreed, though he nevertheless spoke quietly: "Our Scottish King's blown hot and cold with Catholics ever since he came to us two years ago. He's a trickster, if you ask me, making promises and breaking them, hinting and pulling back. He had it coming..."

"I say they were mad to attempt such a thing," said Martin. "And now it's all come home to roost – and brought trouble to us here."

He made a lowering sign with his hands, and all voices dropped. Somewhere outside the room, near the courtyard door, a guard was posted. Master Tandy regularly took care of the guards, supplying them with food and beer, but still we needed to be careful what we said.

"If you ask me," said Barbara, boldly speaking out when the men were in full voice, "they were fools and hotheads, and the young master was a fool to join them, and they've brought nothing but harm to us and to Catholics everywhere. There's Mary here, not knowing what's become of her brother – and him likely to be punished for his loyalty to his master."

"Barbara's right." Martin said. "It was a fool's plan, and now it's crushed it will only bring harsher penalties and make life harder for ordinary Catholics."

"And I wonder how much our young master Francis knew about it – how much he was told," said Barbara. "They've all thrown their lives away for nothing."

I tried to speak then, but only a sound between a gasp and a sob came out.

Barbara was instantly contrite. "Now, Mary, don't fear. They'll spare Rob."

"Come away, Mary," said Mistress Pyatt. "We'll go back to our work."

As the two of us climbed the stairs, she said, "It's a pity that Father Taberer has to be kept hidden, for if the guards were not here we might have all come together for a Mass, and that would have been a comfort, and a healing thing."

But for now we could only wait. The Sheriff of Worcester had called out the posse comitatus, the full force of the county, more than two hundred men. The ports were closed, the whole country was on alert, and both David and Rob were somewhere out there, in danger, while we were prisoners at Lyde Hall.

Chapter Seventeen

"I demand to see my daughter!"

I ran to the window of the sewing room and looked out.

My father was there, at the door, with a horse. He was flushed with anger and venting it on John Frewen, who reluctantly stood firm.

"I can't let you in, master. Nor I can't let anyone out. Sheriff's orders. No visitors, and no one to leave the house until Francis Chilton and Robert Wilshaw be found and taken."

It was early morning on the 14th November. My father must have set off at first light, expecting to take me home.

I raced downstairs and arrived at the door as John was apologising and my father telling him how impossible it was that Rob had committed any crime other than being his master's manservant.

"Dad!"

As soon as I saw my father's face I knew that Thomas Jevons had carried out his threat to send soldiers to search our home and workplace in Dudley. I understood the shock and fear this must have caused, and the shame for a respectable trader of having his premises raided and soldiers everywhere, with neighbours and customers looking on. And now he had come to fetch me, and we could only speak with soldiers listening.

I ran into his arms regardless and we hugged each other on the threshold.

"When did Rob go missing?" he asked. "Your mother is distraught – and to have found out in such a way, with armed men at the door…"

"It all happened in the last few days. I couldn't get out to tell you."

"But they *must* let you come home!"

I warned him with a little shake of the head not to say anything in front of the guard. "Tell Mum I'll come as soon as I can."

Two weeks or so passed before I was able to fulfil my promise. During that time we continued to shelter Father Taberer. Because he had been in hiding when the Sheriff's men came, Father Taberer now had to maintain the fiction that he did not exist. He spent much of his time in the hide for fear one of the guards should see him as they patrolled the house – which they did whenever they were bored or wished to unsettle us. We also had to keep the hide clean and fresh-smelling for fear of betraying its whereabouts, and that created more risk.

Father Taberer celebrated Mass secretly for the two ladies, late at night or in the very early morning. He also heard confession. But we all knew that he could not continue like this and that Thomas Jevons was biding his time and waiting for him to make a mistake and betray himself.

For all of us, our lives at that time felt unreal. All we could do was to wait.

I thought constantly of David. He'd be hiding, perhaps in disguise, somewhere in Kent, waiting till the ports re-opened. I feared for him, but the fear was not as intense and immediate as the fear I now felt for Rob, whose whereabouts and feelings I could not imagine. He was guileless, my brother. He would never have suspected Francis Chilton of being involved in a conspiracy; and his sense of honour would have kept him loyal to his master.

At last, towards the end of November, came the news we had dreaded: that Francis and Rob had been captured. It was the Sheriff's deputy who brought it – the same one we had outwitted so lightly less than two months ago. I saw him arrive, and heard his voice on the floor below as he was admitted to the great chamber.

Later, when he had gone, Jane came to fetch me. I trembled so much that she had to take my arm and support me on the stairs.

I didn't want to face Lady Chilton. I knew her anguish must be much greater than mine, for there could surely be no hope for Francis, and I could not bear the thought of seeing her so grief-stricken. But she had gained command of herself, as I should have known she would, though she was very pale and had lost weight these last weeks. Lady Warne was with her, seated a little way off, a supportive presence.

"Mary," said Lady Chilton, "don't look so fearful.

Your brother is alive and unhurt." She turned to Jane: "Bring Mary a stool."

I breathed in, tried to summon my voice. "Thank you…"

"They were found hiding in a farmer's barn near Penkridge," said the lady. "A servant betrayed them. I know nothing of how…what spirits they are in…" Her voice was husky, and she paused, then continued more clearly, "They are now both in Stafford jail, awaiting examination."

She paused. I wondered what 'examination' meant. Did it mean torture, or the threat of it? I could not endure the thought of Rob being hurt, and I tried to shut it out of my mind.

Lady Chilton continued, "My son will certainly face trial. Your brother, however, may well be freed. We must hope so."

The next day the remaining soldiers left Lyde Hall. We were now free to come and go, though we knew the house would be watched. Lady Chilton had obtained passes for herself and for me to travel to Stafford, since it was outside the five mile limit permitted for recusants.

But first I went home to tell my parents. Henry Gale, who had business in the town, travelled with me. Poor Henry! He didn't know whether to talk to me about Rob, who was causing my family and me such distress, or David, who was lost to me. Instead we talked about lute strings and where one might obtain them in Dudley; and I advised him on the best-priced linen for shirts. And so we parted at the market cross, and he looked at me, anxious and kind, and said, "Take heart, Mary. This will pass."

My parents greeted me with great relief, but talked and fretted over every scrap of news I brought about Rob – which was little enough. Both of them were desperate to see him, and so was Mark, but we doubted whether a family group would be allowed in, so in the end it was my father and I who set off the next day for Stafford. We took gifts of food and clean clothes from my mother, and a promise from us that we would tell her everything – "the truth," she insisted, "even if it be hard to bear."

Stafford is a place I've visited once or twice, on market days, but it's some distance from Dudley and hard going in the short days of late November. It was dark by the time we arrived, and the first thing we did was to find an inn where we could stay the night.

The next morning, early, we went to the prison, only to be told that we could not see Rob. My father protested, but it soon became clear that Rob was not like those who were imprisoned for theft or vagrancy. This was a matter of state security; there had been a plot to kill the king, and Rob was under interrogation.

"For how long?" my father asked.

The guard shrugged. "Till he satisfies the examiners."

All my father could do was to leave the food and clothes and some money, and hope that might buy Rob a bit of comfort, if not mercy.

Then we went home and broke the news to my mother.

Two days later Mark went to Stafford and left more money for Rob's care, but could still find out nothing else except that if Rob was released it was likely to be without warning.

My mother was in such distress she could not eat, yet she carried on the work of the business, dealing with customers when my father was away. Our apprentice Kit, always calm and reliable, kept things running. As for our friends and customers, some offered help, or brought little gifts of food to tempt my mother's appetite, but others stayed away from us, no doubt fearing to be tainted with treason.

My father made another journey to Stafford without seeing Rob, but at last, on a Saturday in early December, my brother arrived home alone on a carrier's cart.

He came in by the back entrance, his hat brim pulled down low over his face. We soon saw why. It wasn't only the bruises and bloodshot eyes, or even the dark weals on his wrist when he raised a hand to remove his hat; it was as if the spirit had gone out of him. He shook, and said he was cold, but we knew it wasn't the cold air.

"Rob, our lad," my mother said, "what have they done to you?"

He flinched when she touched him, either from pain or the fear of it.

She set about getting food ready – recovering instantly now that there was something she could do. "There's broth simmering on the hob," she said, "and bread to sop in it – easy to eat. Mary, give Rob some spiced wine; that'll warm him."

Rob took the cup from me. It rattled against his teeth. "My master is still in prison," he said. His voice was hoarse. Was it from dryness, I wondered, or from shouting, or (I feared even to think it) from screaming? "He'll come to trial after Christmas. They say he was part of the plot, but he – we – never knew anything of that…"

"Don't try to talk," I said. "You're safe home now. We'll get you well."

"But he is still there. Even though they let me go..."
He shivered.

"I'll send for Master Brunt to look you over," my
father said.

Rob shook his head and grimaced. We both had
childhood memories of the apothecary's poultices and bitter
tasting draughts.

"He should come," my father insisted.

Rob nodded. But he seemed unwilling to talk about
what had happened to him.

Gilly came in then, wagging her tail, eager, until she
came closer to Rob; then she snarled, and backed away,
whether from the prison smell or the difference in him
I don't know.

"Gilly, it's Rob," I pleaded, but she was nervous and
would not go to him.

"Give her time," my father said.

Rob ate a little, then washed and went to his chamber
to sleep. In the late afternoon, when the apothecary called
on us, he found Gilly lying protectively beside his patient,
and I had to coax her away.

"He has been hung from his wrists," Master Brunt
reported, when he came downstairs. "His joints and tendons
are stretched; his shoulder was dislocated; a couple of teeth
knocked out; his ribs are badly bruised and two are broken.
But he's young, and will mend." He prescribed poultices for
the bruises, a sleeping draught, and another for the pain.

During Advent, Rob began a partial recovery from most
of the injuries inflicted on him, but he was a changed man.
The jaunty manner and the grin were gone; and his eyes,
that once only had to catch mine to make.me giggle, now

flicked away, dull. It hurt me to see him so diminished.

All our customers gradually returned to the shop. My father was, after all, the best tailor for miles around. But no one quite understood what Rob's involvement in the plot had been; and that, and his changed manner, made people avoid him.

I returned to the sewing room at Lyde Hall, but went home frequently. Rob and my parents needed me, and I wanted to be with them. Once, towards the end of December, I asked Meg if she'd come back with me and bring some remedies – "something to lift the darkness from my brother's spirits." I saw her eyes brighten at the prospect of seeing Rob again, and warned her that he was much changed. But my instinct had been right. He responded well to having Meg visit him rather than old Master Brunt, and I encouraged her to come whenever she could.

All through Christmastide and into January, Lyde Hall seemed to be holding its breath, waiting. Father Taberer had gone – probably to another Catholic household, somewhere distant where he could lie low for a while. The two ladies spent much of their time in private prayer. Mistress Pyatt and I sewed and mended, and I continued my work on the St Winefride banner – though Lady Warne said it might have to be hidden away to await happier times.

All this time I heard nothing of David. I knew only that the ports were now open and he had probably sailed to France. Meg came often to our home in Dudley, and the two of us grew closer. She had Rob to care for, and he was always glad to see her. Between them, Meg and Gilly helped Rob recover; but there was no need for him now in the empty place that Lyde Hall had become, so he stayed on at home, waiting. We were all waiting for news of Francis Chilton's trial.

At last, towards the end of January, it came.

Stephen Littleton of Holbeach House and another of the plotters, who had been on the run together since the 8th November, were betrayed and captured. Those two, along with Francis Chilton, were tried at Stafford, and all three were sentenced to death by hanging: a felon's death. I could not bring myself to pity Francis, but I pitied his mother. Her hair had turned white since November, and her gowns hung so slack that Mistress Pyatt had twice had to take them in and tighten the lacings.

From the start Lady Chilton had insisted that she would go to Stafford and witness her son's execution. "I will not let him face his death alone," she said.

She had no husband to support her on this journey, but her son by marriage – her daughter Anne's husband – travelled from Bedfordshire to take on that role. Master Bagnall the steward and her maid Jane Shenton also accompanied her. They looked a small, lonely party as they set off along the road, dressed entirely in black, but with no visible sign of their faith upon them.

Those of us left behind at Lyde Hall could not hear a mass for Francis Chilton's soul since we now had no priest, but we prayed for the souls of all the condemned men, and for the lady, that she might have peace. Anne and her four small children were with us, so for a while we were busy again and the children's voices brightened the sad house.

Meanwhile, in London, the principal surviving plotters were tried and executed. All were hanged, drawn and quartered in a public spectacle of blood and vengeance.

Rob listened to the details of the plot in bewilderment.

"My master knew none of this," he told us. "He thought they were planning to raise a regiment and needed more men and horses. That man taken at Westminster – Guido Fawkes – he'd been a soldier in Flanders. My master was finding and buying horses for them. They offered him a command post. I thought that if he went to Flanders he'd take me with him; that it would be an adventure."

I believed him. And I saw how Rob would have been caught up in the allure and excitement of such an enterprise, without questioning what was behind it.

We hoped those executions would be the end of the hunt for traitors, but it was only the beginning. All the known recusant houses in the Midlands, including Lyde Hall, were searched again, even more rigorously, and their inhabitants cross-examined. Lady Chilton, still grieving for her son, was forced to submit to a prolonged interrogation over several days. It was as well that Father Taberer had gone, for they knew we had harboured a priest and were determined to find him.

One day, when I was sewing with them, the two ladies began talking of the death in the Tower of London of a Brother Nicholas Owen. When they described him – small, crippled with a hernia – I knew this to be the Brother Nicholas I had met in September; the one who built the hides. I must have made some small sound of shock, because Lady Warne said, "You remember him, Mary?"

"Yes. He came here with the pilgrims on their way to Holywell. He told me the story of St Winefride. I remember him most kindly."

And now he was dead, perhaps from torture. How many more would be caught in this net?

In April two more plotters and a priest were executed at Worcester. And then they captured Father Garnet, the leader of the Jesuits in England – another one I remembered from our evening of music at Lyde Hall. He was found guilty, and in May we heard how he was dragged on a hurdle to St Paul's churchyard to be hanged, drawn and quartered. I thought of the lady, the one Mistress Pyatt had said was his protector, and pitied her.

When I went home for a visit my mother showed me a broadsheet that someone had brought into the shop.

"Do you see this picture, Mary?"

It was an engraving of a single straw of wheat that seemed to show the likeness of a man's face. We read that straw had been laid all around the execution ground where Father Garnet was butchered, and that afterwards people ran forward and seized handfuls of the blood-stained stuff as mementoes. This one straw had been found to bear the priest's image in blood.

"It's a miracle," my mother said on a soft breath.

My father was sceptical, but I wanted to believe. I assured my mother that I'd seen Father Garnet and that the image was a true likeness of him.

That Sunday, in our Protestant church in Dudley, there was of course no mention of the miraculous straw, only thanks for the capture and execution of the king's enemies. We sat in our usual place, among neighbours, but we no longer felt that we were part of the community, accepted by them. Rob brought the taint of treason with him.

All this time, the absence of David lay heavy on me.

It would be four years at least before he could take holy orders, and longer still before he was ready to be sent to England as part of the Jesuit mission. And when he did come, would he look for me? Would we find each other? Sometimes I imagined myself becoming his protector, giving him shelter and keeping him safe, asking nothing else of him. But it was hard to think of David and not think of that other kind of love.

My mother knew something was wrong. One night she came to my chamber as I was preparing for bed. I opened the door to her in my shift, my hair loose and tumbling over my shoulders.

She sat down beside me on the bed.

"What is it, my wench? And don't say 'nothing'" she added, as I opened my mouth. "I know there's something. Not your brother; he's on the mend. So who – or what? Back at Michaelmas you said there was a man…"

I nodded. Tears leaked from my eyes.

"Is he from the Hall?" she asked gently. "Is he in prison?"

"No!" I sniffed and brushed a hand across my face. I'd have to tell her. "No – though he might as well be."

"Who is he?"

"David Hawley. Lady Chilton's secretary."

Her face brightened with approval. "Well, that's—"

"No, it isn't, Mum. He was there in disguise. He's training to be a Jesuit priest. He's gone to France to study and…well, he's gone, and I won't see him again. That's all."

Of course it wasn't all, and she asked if I'd known what he was, and when I said no, not at first, she blamed him; and that made me angry, and I turned away from her and wouldn't talk.

She stayed there while I muffled sobs in my pillow. And then she said, "Lyde Hall must feel empty to you now."

I remembered David at Lyde Hall, how he'd caught my eye right from the start, the tremor of excitement I'd felt every time I saw him, the strategies I'd thought up to meet him, and the rare moments when we were alone together and how alive they made me feel. I had never known anything like that before. And now it was over. David was gone. Lyde Hall was simply a house where I worked – a sad house, full of loss.

She laid a hand on my shoulder. "You *will* get over this, Mary."

I sat up and pushed back my hair. "I don't want to! I don't want to get over him! I don't want to lose him!"

"But you have, my wench. He was never yours. I know it hurts. But it won't always hurt so much. I think, if the lady will spare you, you should have a change – go on a visit. We could go to Alveley, to your aunt Burford, see your cousins..."

I nodded listlessly. I felt little enthusiasm for the idea, though I liked my Burford cousins well enough.

"Think about it," my mother said.

Over the next week or so I did think. I liked the idea of change, but I wanted something more than a visit. And when I thought back over my time at Lyde Hall and all that had happened there, the answer came to me, and I knew what I wanted to do.

Chapter Eighteen

Our first overnight stay was at Shrewsbury. Neither my mother nor I was accustomed to riding long distances, and Rob was not fully recovered from his injuries, so we'd taken it slowly that day.

At first Rob had refused to come, even though he needed this journey more than any of us. He suffered constant pain in his joints – pain that made him feel like an old man, though he'd turned twenty-one only two months ago – but I knew that the main reason was fear of drawing attention to himself, especially fear of encountering soldiers or officials of any kind. Ever since his release from prison he had been living close at home, helping around the shop and yard, but unwilling to venture out. He was very much changed, and I missed the Rob I'd known.

"You were released without charge," I told him. "You are a free man."

But he knew we were planning to travel to a Catholic shrine – one so powerful that the authorities had never been able to destroy it, nor stem the flow of pilgrims.

And the fear and hatred of Catholics was now high in the country; the times were more dangerous than ever.

In the end my mother and I persuaded Rob that we needed him with us to help and protect us on the journey. That roused him better than any talk of his own trouble.

Lady Chilton helped me with my plans and advised me about what to take and where to hire horses.

"I wish I could go," she said, "but this is not the time for me. I have no doubt that Lyde Hall is watched."

"I will pray for you there, my lady, and ask St Winefride for healing for you," I promised.

"And – I beg you – pray for my son's soul," she said. "I will."

She took me into her library and found a map that had belonged to her husband and unrolled it on a table under the window. It was a map of Shropshire and the north-east part of Wales. St Winefride's Well was at Holywell in Wales, a few miles from the coast, and the map showed a route marked with the names of many shrines and ancient places, and the rivers and bridges that lay between them.

"On horseback, in summer, it should not be too long a journey," she said.

I had never travelled so far from home, but ever since the pilgrims had come to Lyde Hall almost a year ago on their way to St Winefride's Well, and Brother Nicholas had told me the saint's story, I had felt a connection to that place. St Winefride, murdered by her rejected suitor and restored to life by her uncle St Beuno, was renowned for her powers of healing. And now I needed healing – not only for myself but for my brother and for Lady Chilton.

Looking at the map, and tracing with a finger the route taken by the pilgrims who had visited Lyde Hall last year, I tried to imagine the miles to Holywell – the people we would meet, the places we would see – and an excitement and a sense of purpose gripped me that I had not felt since David had gone away.

I drew a careful copy, marking in the rivers and bridges, and the names of towns and villages and sacred places along the route: Shrewsbury, Woolston, Oswestry, Llangollen…

Lady Chilton gave me offerings to take on her behalf – small things that my mother and I could hide among our possessions: jewels, a silver crucifix and an illuminated missal with a gold clasp. I brought an altar cloth I had made, embroidered in gold and silver thread.

We left in the third week of June, at a time when the dust from the discovery of the plot was beginning to settle and the executions were over. We did not wish to be recognised as Catholic pilgrims, so travelling as a group of three people with no obvious signs of piety seemed wise. The first stage of our journey was one we had all made before on several occasions, since Shrewsbury was a centre for the trade in woollen fabrics. But it also had meaning for us as Catholics. Long ago the bones of St Winefride had been brought to Shrewsbury Abbey and a shrine built for her there. This had been destroyed in the time of King Henry, and the precious bones lost, all but one finger bone. The abbey was a ruin – a sad reminder to us now of all the trouble we had suffered. It was late when we arrived, and we were tired, so with our minds on the day ahead we found an inn and took rooms there, and ate a simple supper.

I thought about David that evening, remembering that he came from Shrewsbury and that his parents perhaps lived nearby. I had not thought of him so much lately.

It was now more than seven months since we'd parted, and the sharpness of loss had blunted. And yet I was unwilling to let go of my grief; it would seem disloyal, as if I had never really loved him. Safe in a pocket under my skirts was my needle case with the torn-off scrap of his letter to me still inside it. I knew, without looking, what it said: '...*will endeavour to do the same, dear Mary, though I love you and always will. D.H.*' I knew it was a sin to be taking it with me on this journey of repentance, but I could not bring myself to destroy it.

Next morning we headed north-west out of the town. It was midsummer, and until we left Shrewsbury we'd had fair weather. All around us in the fields men had been at work scything the hay, while women helped spread it out to dry and children scurried around, gathering the stray stalks. But now, as we struck out into the countryside, rain came sweeping across the fields – fine, small rain that penetrated clothing and baggage and half-blinded us as we urged our horses onward. We heard shrieks and shouts as the reapers ran with cloths to cover the cut grass. It seemed a bad omen.

The rain continued all morning, and when we arrived at a wayside alehouse in a hamlet along the way, we were drenched and cold. The woman of the house welcomed us in, offering beer and a slice of meat pie; and, while Rob went to see to the horses, she and our mother talked of the interrupted haymaking and the trials of travelling on horseback. Two young men sat nearby, talking in low voices. One of them, from the way she spoke to him, I guessed was the woman's son.

Rob came in as our mother was asking the woman the way to Woolston, where there is a sacred well.

"Straight on for about a mile, then take the left turn, and when you come to a crossroads, turn left, then right. The lanes twist this way and that, but you'll find it." She eyed the three of us, sizing us up, and I noticed that the two men had stopped talking. "Travelling to Holywell in Wales, are you? Pilgrims?"

Rob, beside me, tensed. But my mother said yes, we were, and the woman nodded and began telling us about a journey she'd made there, long ago. The two young men stood up and went out together, the door opening briefly on a gust of rain and wind.

Later, in the stable, as we were leaving, Rob turned to our mother. "You took a chance there – telling her our business."

"Oh! She seemed a kindly soul. And she'd guessed."

"Maybe. But we were overheard."

We rode out, glad to find that the rain had lessened.

We took the left turn as instructed, reached a crossroads, and paused to look about us. The trees and bushes were high and in full leaf, turning the roads into narrow green tunnels, and we nearly missed the milestone marked 'Woolston' half buried in nettles.

"This way," said Rob – but as he rode forward I heard fast hoof beats, turned and saw two men on horseback burst from the narrow lane to my right.

"Rob!" I cried – too late. They made straight for him and knocked him from his horse. My own horse reared and almost threw me. I dismounted awkwardly, wrenching my right shoulder, and scrambled away from the hooves. As I rose to my feet I saw Rob spring up. His hand went straight to his dagger, but even as he drew it the men were upon him. One struck him a blow with a cudgel; the other kicked away the dagger, knocked him down again and beat him with his fists.

The one with the cudgel saw me and yelled, "Give us your purse and we'll let him go!"

I heard a scream from our mother. She was down from her horse now and came running to defend Rob, who was struggling to rise.

The man with the cudgel caught her and flung her aside. "Your purse! Now!"

"Mum! Stay back!" I warned. And to the men I shouted, "Leave him! I'll give you the money!"

I knew it would be useless to resist. I opened my pack and brought out a purse. We had several between us, on our bodies as well as one in each pack. The first man (he had a scarf tied around his face, but I was sure he was one of those from the alehouse) seized it, then came and rummaged in the pack. He ignored the silver crucifix, but snatched up Lady Chilton's ruby necklace, stuffing that and the purse quickly away under his clothes.

Then, in a moment, they were gone, vanished into the maze of lanes and high summer greenery.

Rob was on his feet, casting about for his dagger, which had fallen into a ditch. He had a black eye and a bloody nose and probably bruised ribs as well. He was furious with himself and almost in tears at having failed to protect us, and our mother was distraught at the sight of his injuries and afraid that his ribs, so newly healed, might have been broken again.

"Mum, if Rob's hurt, it's your fault!" I exclaimed. I was still shaking from the shock of the assault. "If you hadn't been so full of talk—"

"Don't you dare scold me, Mary! I said no more than any civil traveller might—"

"Those men were the two from the alehouse," I said. "All three were probably in league together: she tells us the way; they come up a quicker route to ambush us—"

Rob turned on me. "Leave Mum be, will you?"

"Rob, *you* told her back there she'd been careless! We'd agreed not to speak of a pilgrimage. And now you're hurt and I've lost Lady Chilton's rubies—"

"Yes – because you opened the pack and let him see them! Why didn't you give him the purse from your pocket?"

"I didn't think. How *could* I – with the other one beating you? He had his eye on the pack, so I opened it."

"Will you two stand here quarrelling all day?" demanded our mother. "Rob, you're hurt—"

"No, I'm not, Mum," he said, "not badly. But we need to get away from this place and find the well."

I nodded, abashed. "We do."

The well at Woolston is a place where St Winefride's bones rested when they were carried from Holywell to Shrewsbury. Since that time pilgrims have found peace there. We could not approach it with our hearts full of anger.

We rounded up and calmed the horses, and Rob helped our mother to mount; then we set off along the lane. A short distance away we came upon a cluster of cottages. Some women there nodded to us in a friendly manner, but our trust in people had been shaken and we passed through the hamlet quickly, turned north, and came soon after to the holy well.

It was small – a spring and well in a shady place with a stone basin built around it. We entered the little chapel on the bank above, and knelt and prayed, bringing our thoughts back to the purpose of our journey. We were seen, of course, as we arrived, and when we left an old woman came out of a cottage nearby and told us she was the keeper of the shrine. She looked at Rob's battered face, but said nothing about it and offered no help. We gave her some coins and she set us on our way to Oswestry, where we hoped to find an inn for the night.

We stopped short of the town at a wayside inn. By that time all three of us were feeling the effects of injuries and shock. We were glad to dismount and leave the horses in the care of the ostlers and go inside.

My mother and I had a little room high under the eaves. It was cramped, but at least we didn't have to share the bed with other travellers. We took turns washing in the basin of water. My shoulder felt stiff and painful, and my mother rubbed it with a salve she'd brought with her.

"I hope our Rob's safe tonight," she said. "He took such a beating from those rogues."

We got into bed and blew out the candle, and in the darkness I put my arms around her and said, "I'm sorry I shouted at you, Mum."

"No matter, my wench. We were angry and hurt. Tomorrow will be better."

But in the morning we found that all three of us were covered in flea bites. And outside the sky was dark and full of rain clouds.

The clouds burst soon after we left Oswestry. As we headed north, day after day, the ground rose higher and it was harder going. This bleak mountainous country was like nothing I had ever experienced before, and the vast unforgiving emptiness of it terrified me. Often we dismounted and led the horses up steep stony paths, seemingly endless. Or we rode in the valleys along rain-slippery grassy trails with mountains looming above us. The sky was huge, the countryside wild and empty, with scattered farm houses the only sign of human life. We passed a great waterfall, a ruined abbey, and a strange stone pillar that appeared suddenly out of the mist. This stone was covered with writing that Rob said was Latin, though it was greatly weathered.

"It's a monument to some old king," he said.

But in that wild place the pillar oppressed me with a fear of ghosts and demons and ancient haunted sites. There were springs and small Christian shrines along the route, but with the rain beating in our faces and slowing us down we did not linger long at these but continued doggedly on our way. Sometimes we met other travellers, and there were pilgrims like us at the inns where we stayed overnight; but much of the time we were alone, cut off from others by rain and mist. Despite everything, I was determined to reach St Winefride's shrine, no matter how hard the journey. At times it seemed that we would be lost in the mountains forever, but there was always a path – often narrow, meandering and rocky, but still a path. Its presence there gave me hope.

And the rain did ease, as we came down into gentler country; and at last we came to Holywell and stopped at an inn on the edge of town. Here, for the first time, we would be clearly recognisable as Catholic pilgrims, and would need to be careful. I could see that Rob was nervous already. I had heard that innkeepers here were under orders to keep names and addresses of all their visitors, and I guessed that in these dangerous times the lists would be collected and scrutinised regularly by the authorities. But many innkeepers refused to comply and, besides, who would know if you gave a false name? So we did that, and retired to our chambers.

An hour later we removed our shoes and stockings and set off to walk the last mile barefoot to St Winefride's shrine.

The stones of the road hurt my feet, but this barefoot walk was the custom and I wanted to do it. It was a long mile, and painful, and my feet were soon cut and bruised, but after a while the pain seemed less, and I felt I was gaining strength with every step. I looked at my mother and brother, and saw them bravely picking their way along the road – all of us part of a growing crowd of people moving slowly towards the shrine. Some were frail, some old, many on crutches, some carrying sickly children, some with withered or missing limbs.

We came first to the courtyard and the outer pool, where we saw pilgrims bathing. Beyond this open-air space, the shrine and well were enclosed by a tall two-storey building like a church. Its grandeur astonished me after the little sacred wells and springs we had passed on our way here. A high columned chamber, open to the air, surrounded a star-shaped pool. Its roof was carved with symbols, and the light that filtered through it was greenish and dappled with reflections from the water. It was beautiful; and all around I saw initials and messages carved on the columns by those who had received the saint's blessing. But the alcove where her statue should have been was empty, the stone left hacked out and broken.

We made our gifts to the shrine, and prayed, then went to bathe. Men and women bathed separately, and

Rob left us, while my mother and I entered a room where we took off our outer clothes and ventured out dressed only in our shifts. Despite the sunshine we were shivering.

Each in turn we went to the front of the well and made our intentions. Mine were to atone for my sin with David and to pray for healing for my brother, Lady Chilton, and the soul of Francis Chilton. I had thought deeply about those I was to pray for. It was not difficult to ask God's blessing for those I loved. For Francis Chilton it was harder as I cared nothing for this man who had been the cause of so much grief to us all; but I had made a promise to his mother and hoped my pity for her would help me pray for her son.

Now I recited the Apostles' Creed and one decade of the rosary while walking around the well; and then I went outside and down the steps into the water of the outer pool, gasping as I felt its cold shock. I took a breath and immersed myself. I rose with dripping hair, my shift tangling around my legs. Down I plunged again, before I lost courage; and a third time, rising up in a shower of spray. Then I moved, weighted with water, to the stone they call St Beuno's Stone, and knelt there and prayed, the air icy on my wet skin. Despite my shivering, I felt strong, tingling, alive.

Afterwards, dry and dressed, my mother and I put on our shoes, met up with Rob, and walked back to the inn. That evening we attended a secret Mass in one of the upper rooms. I had almost been afraid to go to this Mass, and Rob looked haunted with fear; but we did go, and I was glad we had found the courage, for I felt we would need it in the times to come.

*

Our return journey was very different to the outward one. The rain had eased while we were at Holywell, and now the sun's warmth and light and the long evenings made travelling easier. We lingered on the way and visited some of the shrines and churches I had marked on my map, and sometimes stepped away from the direct path altogether.

One afternoon Rob and I left our mother resting near the tethered horses and climbed up a steep hillside, scrambling over rocks and tussocks, crossing twisting sheep trails. I stumbled over my long skirts, and he reached back and hauled me up.

The wind slammed into us at the summit.

"Rob," I gasped, "your injuries – you'll hurt—"

"Look!" he said.

I looked out to the west and saw mountains, blue-grey and misty, mountains beyond mountains, on into the distance.

We stared, panting, triumphant, then laughed and hugged each other. I had not seen him smile since he came out of prison.

"Are you healed?" I asked. "Has St Winefride made you whole again?"

"The pain is still there," he said. "It hurt me to climb – but I had to do it." He shot me a glance, oddly shy. "Told Meg I'd climb a mountain for her."

Meg. So something *had* come of that. I felt a glow of pleasure. He'd begun venturing out a little these last few months, since his injuries had begun to heal, giving Meg less reason to visit. He never went far. And I'd guessed – hoped – it might be to call at her home near Lyde village.

"She'll be proud of you," I said.

"I hope so."

"What will you do when we get home? You won't go back to Lyde Hall?"

"No, never!" he said, with such vehemence that I wished I hadn't asked.

"But you'll need to find work."

"Yes. But gentlemen always need servants, and merchants need salesmen. A cloth merchant might take me on. And you? What will *you* do, our wench?"

"I don't think I'll stay much longer at Lyde Hall. There was a rumour going around that Lady Chilton might go to live with one of her daughters, and the Hall be let."

"Dad would be glad to have you back in the business."

I nodded. Being back home would do for a while, I thought, especially if I could continue with my embroidery. I had a few regular customers already in the town, and I thought there must surely be a market for fine work among the gentry.

We turned away from the mountains and looked down the way we had come, at the road, and our mother, small and alone.

"Going down will be harder," said Rob. He grinned.

A sheep bleated nearby. We moved, startling it, and it skittered away, its ragged woolly rump bounding along a narrow track. I bunched up my skirts and we began the descent with shouts, shrieks and slithering falls. We arrived next to our mother, play-fighting and teasing each other and breathless with laughter. It was like the old days at home.

The next morning we visited one of the churches

we'd missed on our hard outward journey. It was near Llangollen, a church with a carved wooden ceiling that made me cry out in delight: it was decorated all over with lions and serpents, roses, vines, and angels. I walked around, gazing at that ceiling for a long time, absorbing the intricacy of the design and workmanship.

Later we wandered among the ruins of the monastery we had seen on our way north, and now I no longer noticed its destruction but saw the power of what was left: the great arch with its window spaces, empty of glass, standing open to the sky and the light.

I knew I would remember this journey all my life.

On our last day, riding home from Shrewsbury, we passed a group of merchants travelling in the opposite direction, and they nodded to us in greeting as travellers do on the road. One of them, a young man with an open, pleasing face, looked at me, and our eyes met, briefly, before I lowered mine.

They were strangers, gone in an instant. But I realised then that there would be other journeys ahead of me. Marriage. Children, if I was blessed. I would love another man. And although I would never forget David, I knew he was on a journey of his own. My love for him would fade, and become a memory: the last secret from that time at Lyde Hall, and the one I would always keep.

Author's Note

When the Gunpowder Plot was discovered in London, in early November 1605, several of the core plotters fled to their homes in the Midlands, and the final drama was played out at Holbeach House near Kingswinford. Many great houses in the Midlands were home to Catholic recusants, and these were places where Jesuit priests – and also young men on their way to study at Jesuit colleges in France – were sheltered and hidden from the authorities.

Lyde Hall is imaginary, and so are the Chilton family and everyone else who lives there. But nearby Holbeach House is a real place, and in 1605 its owner, Stephen Littleton, was involved on the fringes of the Gunpowder Plot. I have given my imaginary character Francis Chilton a similar link to the plot – or at least the suspicion of being involved.

A pilgrimage to St Winefride's shrine at Holywell by people close to the plot really did take place in early September 1605. It is known that these pilgrims stayed at several great houses along their way, and since my imaginary Lyde Hall was on their route I have given them an additional stay there.

Brother Nicholas Owen, who designed and built many of the priests' hides in Catholic houses, died in the Tower of London in 1606, almost certainly from torture. He was made a saint in 1970.